THE URBAN SAMURAI SERIES
BOOK 2

N.S. KELLY

DEDICATIONS

From Book 1: Thank you to **Deidre Knight** who mentioned something about wanting to read a story about female samurai during a RWA conference one time. From her comment, Shia and her sisters were born. Of course, they took a totally different turn than I intended!

To **our son**, who gets that some nights are just writing nights and some days, we have to work out the logic of our stories or his.

Tee & Pip, Thank you for your creative souls, friendship and crazy podcast nights. Well, and everything else!

Claudia LeFeve - for the recommendation of going backwards through the books, you are a gem.

To Stacia's Sparkling Hearts crew, **JT, Elizabeth & Kate (Cat)** - I am seriously forever grateful for meeting each and every one of you and for your support and mad skills.

CHAPTER 1

"You'll never take me alive, coppers!"

Detective Ryan Calder dropped to the cold ground as lasers fired over his head. He'd flanked and cornered his suspect, but this one had a guile and wit reserved for only the craftiest foes. "Give it up, Danger. We've got you surrounded!"

His target replied with a snort and a laugh. "Don't be a fool. I've already shot down your partner. You're next." It was true. Danger had gotten the drop on Ryan's partner, finishing him off when they chased him into the suburban backyard. Backup wasn't coming, and if Ryan didn't think quickly, he'd be finished too.

"There's still time for you to turn yourself in. Use your head or it's over for you."

"How 'bout you stand up and take it like a man, cop? I've got you pinned down, and I can wait here all day long."

Ryan reached down and untied his boot, leaving it in place. Then he crawled on his belly on the frosty lawn. He inhaled and exhaled through his nose to minimize the visibility of his breath in the winter air. "Last chance, Danger." He heard his target's slow footsteps moving closer and knew he was losing leverage.

The footsteps grew quicker, and then Danger pounced, appearing in Ryan's field of view. He stood triumphantly over Ryan's vacant boot, laser rifle aimed to finish off the detective. Instead, Ryan squeezed off two shots, hitting his target square in the chest.

"Player Two – Game Over."

"Aww, man," the dejected kid called Danger groaned as his Laser Danger chest piece went from green to red. He moved his gaze to Ryan, frustration set all over his head and shoulders.

Ryan tsk'ed and rose to his feet. "Good game, kiddo, maybe you'll get me next time."

"That's what you said last time."

"Yep," Ryan nodded, "and it's probably what I'll say next time. Now, be a good kid and throw your uncle his shoe. My toes are goin' numb."

Curled up in the pool of sunshine streaming through the dirty windows of the old warehouse, she stared down at the old leather book in her hands. She should head back to the current place she called home. They'd be calling the cops on her soon. She'd skipped school and instead wandered around the city, people-watching all day.

She wrapped her cold fingers around the leather bound edges. She'd never thought she'd be able to do the things she'd been able to do in the last week. All because she'd wandered into the old bookstore and found the thing hiding on a back shelf, drawn to it as she'd never been drawn to anything before. The oddity of it all, her in a bookstore. Her newest foster parents would swear she'd never cracked open a book, much less knew how to read. She knew much more than that now, so much more. Her black lacquered nails looked garish against the fragile pages. She'd learned quickly to be gentle with the pages because of how easily they crumbled. She'd lost one page that way already.

Her finger trailed over the page, the words blurring, then righting themselves in English. She wasn't sure what the original language had been, but every time she focused on a page, it shifted and then righted itself before her eyes. She'd show them. Her foster parents whispered about her behind her back, sometimes to her face. The newest ones, she'd been with them, maybe three months, maybe less, seemed nice enough. She couldn't wait for her 18th birthday to get her out of the system and out on her own. She'd been looking for a new place to live when she'd found the old bookstore. She'd wandered into it, hidden in a back alley in Chinatown. Another day she should have been in school.

Job hunting and home hunting. She wanted a place of her own and people of her own, not the ones Social Services kept throwing her. The wind ripped through the warehouse sending the book's pages flipping. An old can clattered across the cement floor. She turned to make sure it was only the wind, when she turned back, the words swirled on the new page. Words leapt up at her. As she read, her heart began to beat faster.

Supplies. She'd need supplies. Finally, something to help her make the changes she longed to. She shut the book as gently as she could and tucked it back in her black backpack. No need to carry the fragile thing in her arms. She stood and made a quick mental calculation.

Back to Chinatown for supplies before heading home. Hopefully, her foster parents hadn't already called the cops on her. Maybe things could go her way for once.

Ryan took a sip off of his coffee, checking his phone for missed messages. Today was his first day off since the whole incident with Spiros and the demons. He'd missed Thanksgiving, but homicides didn't care what the schedule on the wall said. He tried to make it up today with the visit to his sister and her family. He felt the glare of said sibling and tried not to smirk.

"You took your boot off? My stars, Ryan, how competitive are you?"

"I don't like to lose, sis. You know that better than anyone."

"Really, Ry?" The detective looked up to meet his sister's brown eyes. Chloe "CC" Calder-Williams gave him the same look she had ever since they were kids. The smirk finally crossed Ryan's face. All grown up with a husband, kids and a house of her own, and she was still his baby-faced little sister.

"Okay, okay," Ryan shrugged, "I'll let him beat me in Gruden Football next time I visit."

CC waved a finger at her brother. "You'd better."

Danny Williams, CC's husband, emerged from the back of the house, towel-drying his hair. "Hey, it's good for the kid to lose every once in a while."

She was outnumbered, but not outsmarted. "You're just glad your team won. If not for your 'partner' over here, you and DJ would already be on your way to the toy store."

Danny smiled. "I'll take him anyway." He kissed his wife on the cheek.

"I know," she replied, pulling him back for a quick kiss on the lips.

Ryan grinned and picked up his coffee. His baby sister was living the American dream. House in the suburbs, complete with two kids, PTA, and the church choir. She and Danny were in love and still managed to show it with two children underfoot and his grueling government contractor job. If things had been different, maybe he could have wound up in that life. Then again, with what he knew, he was certain a "normal" life wasn't a possibility. "Sounds like a fun trip."

Danny grabbed the coffee pot, pouring himself a cup. "You want to tag along? Plenty of room in the Soccer Mom mobile."

"Thanks, but I can't. I have to get back." He put his empty mug in the sink and patted Danny on the back. "Next time, partner."

CC rolled her eyes and hugged her brother. "You can't leave without saying goodbye to the kids."

Ryan's exchange with his niece and nephew was much less personal. The playroom, which CC kept meticulous when the kids were in school, looked like it was hit by a tornado. Madison was nestled in a corner in a pile of dolls, reading a book to them. Danny "DJ" Williams, Junior, aka "Danger", had cleared the center of the room and was focused on the video screen. His arms flailed in the air as he played his favorite video game, Gruden Football 2016.

"Okay, guys, I'm out of here." Madison looked up long enough to wave goodbye and blow a kiss. DJ half-grunted a goodbye over his shoulder. Ryan shook his head. Each of the kids was a carbon copy of their parents. With a smile firmly planted on his face, the detective walked back out of the playroom and out of the Williams' home sweet home.

The V8 engine of the Impala roared to life as he approached the car. Brushing some snow from his shoulders, Ryan opened the door and dropped into the driver's seat. "Well, that was subtle. Couldn't wait till I got in the car?"

The slightly electronic voice of the artificial intelligence replied in a confused tone. "I was certain you wanted the car warmed up upon your arrival."

"Yeah, that was a nice touch, Jace," Ryan replied. "However, cars don't have a proximity sensor or trigger based on their owner's body temperature."

"I have adjusted the Impala to be capable of both functions, as well as..."

"Jace."

"Yes, sir?"

"Stow it. Call your boss. I'm sure she's worried sick about you."

Dr. Zenshi Jin Ronin, Shia to most, barely glanced at the incoming call flashing on her screen. She was still several shades of irritated at Jace, her AI, who had so rudely accepted Detective Ryan Calder into their battles without her knowing or approval. Not that she wasn't thankful for the sexy Detective's help in the battle with the Rissu demon, but she preferred to keep human interactions with the other realms as limited as possible. Instead, she forced herself to focus on the several screens she now had set up on her desk in the home office.

Since she'd moved back into the warehouse, she'd fully committed to designing the surrounding buildings she'd purchased years ago. The outsides of the three other buildings remained untouched except those areas that were needed for structural safety. Inside, new hardwoods gleamed, office spaces, training spaces and even space for vehicles. Jace designed a state of the art security system, shielding everything inside the small area from satellite detection, keeping them effectively hidden from prying eyes around the world. She might not be able to block out the other realms, but she'd become very adept at hiding in the human one. She'd built a sanctuary for herself and her sisters, having a nagging feeling that things were going to get much worse before they got better.

The screen to her left blinked again, this time, Ilsa's beautiful blond visage flashed with her name. The gorgeous Scandinavian helped to manage the business end of things for the Samurai sisters. Eleven of them spanned the globe each demon hunting in her own territory. Shia tapped the screen and opened up the connection to the only other woman even remotely close to her in age.

"Ignoring me?" Ilsa smiled at her. The plush leather office behind her resonated with all the vibrancy of the finer things in life. For the most part, the Samurai weren't lacking in material goods or technology, which hadn't always been the case.

"No, Jace, I'm ignoring." She tapped close on the incoming call from the AI again. She'd turned off all his communication paths in the office. She turned back to the others screens giving Ilsa a side view of her face. "He's gotten a little away from his programming."

"I can't believe how much you rely on technology nowadays. There was a time." Ilsa said.

Shia slanted her a look and then went back to her screens. "Times change. The wise person learns to adapt."

Data streamed past her eyes, news reports from around the nation. Commentaries on blogs, videos and more. She stopped trying to absorb all of it at once, instead focusing on letting something stand out and demand her attention.

"Have they returned yet?" Ilsa asked, her face turning to the side, the sounds of a keyboard clicking away on the other side of the world.

"They'll be traveling by normal means, and she's had to hide the child so they both can heal. They'll bc hcrc in due time." Shia sighed. Shellie, the North American Samurai had disappeared tracking a Rissu demon and child a few weeks ago. She wasn't going to rush their return and do more harm than good to the young one who'd be entering their domain. "Do you want to do the honors of creating a link for the child or shall I?"

"Let me build a background for her. Since Shellie found her, we should likely make her the young one's relation." Ilsa smiled. "She more of a mothering type than any of the rest of us."

Shia smiled, "True. And she'll love having the little one underfoot." Shia clicked a few more buttons and tapped on the screen sending out orders to the others. They needed to know they had a new and future sister in their ranks.

She swiveled her chair back to face Ilsa. "We really should call a family meeting."

"True. We need to figure out funding, do supply checks and see about getting Shellie and the child home safely." Ilsa twisted her long blonde hair up and secured it with a claw. "We'll start calling them to you over the next few days."

"Agreed." Another chime rang out around the office space. Shia laughed. "Impatient AI doesn't like me keeping him blocked from talking to me. I'll let you know when they arrive. I've got to get on scene."

Ilsa smiled. "Enjoy."

Shia grinned back at her, a rare grin. "Oh, I always do." She winked and tapped the screen closed before clicking the other call open.

"Lady."

Shia cut him off before he could begin. "Shellie will eventually be making her way home with the child. You may have fun changing the warehouse next door to suit Shellie, a five year old, and perhaps a Shifter or two."

She wouldn't leave anything to chance with the way men had been appearing in their realm lately. Adapt to change. "I've being called in to deal with a dead body. I'll reopen your comm channels if you promise to remember to play nice and inform me of any updates."

"I will start the modifications right away. And, I was playing nicely as you put it. You've programmed me to keep you safe and use any means necessary." If an artificial intelligence could sound put out, hers did. "What dead body?"

Shia shook her head at the screen and tapped a few more buttons before standing. Lights began turning on and off as she trailed through the warehouse. The AI's voice now followed her as well.

"I don't know what dead body yet. I was just called in. Dead body in Franklin Park, corner of 14th and K Street. I'll get the details when I'm there." She stepped into her large walk in closet. "I'll snag the comm for my ear before I leave."

"I'll have the car ready to go." Jace chimed.

She switched her focus and quickly changed into better gear for her job. Her sword sheathes hidden and strapped across her back. Thank god most people refrained from touching her, but she wasn't about to wander around the city without her weapons again. The last encounter left some scars.

A few less visible than others.

CHAPTER 2

"Dr. Ronin, glad you could get here so quickly." An officer, she didn't know his name and didn't get a glimpse of his badge fast enough, lifted up the crime scene tape to let her under it.

She nodded and ducked under, murmuring a soft thank you and shouldered her camera bag on one side and the ME Kit on the other. She'd been called out more and more often lately. Her team stretched thin across the District. She'd rather do her work in the lab, but sometimes the guys in black needed her on scene more. She'd been out a week chasing the Mother Rissu demon and her boys, so she owed it to her staff to put in some of their street time rather than hers. Not to mention, she wanted to make sure there were no lingering effects from the Rissu lurking about. Too bad it couldn't have been about ten degrees warmer.

She shuddered even in the warmth of her coat. "Was around the corner. No worries."

She hadn't been, but the officer didn't need to know that.

"The body is right over there." He pointed in a general direction, his eyes going back to the people jockeying for best position on the other side of the tape.

14

Shia frowned as she set one foot in front of the other in the snowy darkness towards the direction the officer indicated. He didn't offer to guide her over, certain he'd been assigned a post and nothing more.

Something tingled on the edge of her awareness, but she couldn't place it. Nothing leapt out at her as wrong or otherworldly, but there was something dancing on the edges. She pulled out her phone and tapped out a quick message to Jace and dropped it back in her pocket.

She'd use all the resources she had to her advantage.

The Impala's engine roared loud enough to drown out the gathering tourists and onlookers. The alternating red and blue of the lights reflected off of the dusting snow. Ryan parked half-way on a curb, close enough to ruin the camera shot of a local reporter. He'd never been fond of reporters. After his last case, he'd begun to outright despise all of them.

He exited the car, pulled the collar of his coat up, and approached the crime scene. A mustached sergeant, yelling at his patrolmen for their slow pace sealing off the area, stopped long enough to acknowledge him. "Sorry to drag you out here on such a lovely night, detective."

Ryan nodded. "Not your fault, O'Shaughnessy. I blame the killer."

"We aren't sure there is a killer, detective, just a body." The older cop replied.

"O'Sho," Ryan answered, "there's a body. You don't call homicide if it's another frozen homeless guy who left this world under the statue of John Barry. You call if there's a possible murder, and we've never built a solid case against Jack Frost yet."

"Nice guess," O'Shaughnessy said, gesturing with a thumb over his shoulder. "Right over there. The ME beat you to the scene by a few minutes. Losing your touch, lead foot."

Ryan grunted an acknowledgement and walked toward the west side of the park. Franklin Square was a block away from the White House. If a murder had been committed here, there would certainly be video. He was mentally cutting through the red tape for warrants and chain-of-custody orders when he arrived at the body. Maybe Jace would be good for something after all.

Portable LED floodlights filled Franklin Square with more brilliance than a pro football game. Sprinkles of snow peppered the spotlights and melted once they touched down. From his perspective, Ryan could see the vic's body spread eagle on the ground beneath the statue of Commodore John Barry.

Once he got a clear view of the victim, he knew why the regular beat cops hadn't hesitated to contact homicide. The vic was a Caucasian male, probably late teens. He sported ripped up jeans, white Converse sneakers, and a spiked leather jacket, all the rage among modern high schoolers. His shoulder length hair and black eyeliner would have been easier to recognize if his skull was still attached.

The vic's neck had been all but severed. His skull was pulled back, nearly touching the back of his jacket. His mandible was still shot forward. Ryan thought of the scene in Alien, where the extraterrestrial life form rips out of Harry Dean Stanton's chest. This something, whatever it was, had erupted out of the vic's mouth, breaking his neck and splitting his skull in the process.

The ME on the case sported a full parka. At the moment, he was hovering over the body, snapping images with a high definition camera. Ryan approached from behind, pulling his collar tight to his neck. "Wow. Quite a mess, huh?

The form before him tensed slightly, and then continued with snapping pictures, "Yes, Detective. Quite the mess. And, quite the power. Please don't step on my crime scene."

Ryan recognized the voice, and the movement of the form before him. He mentally cursed for missing it earlier.

"Shi..." he started, then stopped.

Shia Ronin, medical examiner, samurai, warrior who saved him from death more than once. He'd last seen her, a few days ago, in Little Falls Park battling the large lobster like creature, the Mother Rissu demon. He'd been shuffling around for the last few days wondering how he was going to reach out to her after all the upheaval. He coughed, shifted on his boots, then fell back on the emotionless cadence he'd learned in the Air Force, and later the Police Academy.

"Dr. Ronin, what have you found so far?" He asked.

The form before him stilled before moving to another angle to snap another picture. Low to the ground, she shifted, almost dance in motion.

"I'm still processing. Detective, why don't you tell me what you see while I'm gathering data," she said.

Ryan shook his head, moving his eyes from her form to the victim. She caught him looking, as usual. If anyone could have eyes in the back of her head, it was her. She had the uncanny ability to be looking away from him, yet seeing every little thing he did. He looked back at the disfigured victim, trying to center his focus, and training, on the corpse lying in the frosted grass.

"Caucasian male, maybe eighteen. Cause of death looks like mutilation. Acute stress to the neck and spinal cord resulting in asphyxiation. Someone tried to and managed to take part of this kid's head off."

"Agreed - jaw ripped from his head – let's not sugar

coat it." Shia answered and shifted her position.

She had no reason to hide, cover up or change what so many could see. Too many eyes here now, he knew she couldn't even if she wanted to.

She finished up with her camera and turned to her medical bag and pulled out several syringes. Ryan watched her. She never looked up to face him. That wasn't by chance or on accident. He could reach for her shoulder in an attempt to get her attention, but he wasn't keen on getting his wrist broken.

"If you were going to separate my jaw from my skull, you'd take the jaw, right? Why keep the jaw in place and sever the skull from the spine?" He asked instead. He stopped, still watching her ignore him. "And how the hell do you even make that happen?"

Shia stopped snapping pictures, "You are correct. It takes a powerful force or ..."

"Or a very targeted strike," Ryan replied. "I'm thinking we need to start targeting local dojos. What's your expert opinion?"

She tilted her angle, "Let's take a shot at both? I can't tell you if it was rage, a crime of passion or anything else yet."

"I've studied plenty of techniques aimed at the throat, or the nose, but never any move meant to drive the skull backward so hard. You know more...of more arts than I do. Ever seen or read something like this?" Ryan asked.

Shia slanted him a look. "Someone very strong with a very powerful intent." He knew she could have said more, but left it at that. "I'll need to analyze the samples."

Her phone buzzed, loud enough for them both to hear.

"Funny, I turned that off." She glanced down at the screen and nodded to herself.

He watched her take a deep breath before she stepped closer and flipped the screen so he could see it.

A dark map with heat signatures glowed up at them.

Ryan frowned. "That what I think it is?"

"Yes," she said. He noticed she bit the edge of her lip. Red dots danced around the scene, the blue showed the corpse. What stood out was the faint orange glow surrounding the blue corpse, which trailed away, faintly, very faintly, but there enough for Jace to have picked it up and sent it to her.

Apparently, by her body language, not an aura she could visibly see.

"So, we're dealing in your realm, after all?"

Shia's realm was the supernatural, not only science and death. She wasn't just the medical examiner. She was a samurai who spent centuries hiding in human skin, slaying demons, and protecting innocents. Her world defied explanation. Ryan had been introduced to it on their last case, when his homicide victim wound up a human sacrifice.

"Got a plan, Dr. Ronin?" He asked.

"It's not something I detected, but the computer." She frowned staring off into the darkness where the faint orange trails led on the computer screen. She looked as though she wanted to set off after the trails she could see via the map on her phone. "I need to analyze the scene first. I can only hope this is the only call to a scene tonight."

"You have a smart phone, Detective?" She asked as she turned, finally looking up at him.

He half-grinned down at her, ready to be lost in her eyes. "I do, and a smart car."

Shia frowned at him. "A smart car?" She held up a hand. "No, I don't want to know."

His phone buzzed, startling them both.

She sighed as if giving up on some task. "I'm guessing you now have a physical trail to follow while I do the science magic."

Ryan bit back a smile. Damn Jace, the darn AI knew she'd rather be on the trail, but needed data first. Both he and the AI knew the fact that she couldn't detect the trail on her own bothered her. As if they both weren't in hot water with her to begin with.

Ryan nodded. "The ground's frosty enough that his path should be easy to track. I'll get a team working on expanding the crime scene and looking for any signs of other folks with him. Most of the buildings on the east side of the square are historic, but there are a few law offices here on the west. That means security cameras, and, if there was anything really dramatic, I can check with the White House. Anything that went south would certainly trip the auto-cannons on the roof before reaching the grounds."

Shia nodded. "Sounds like a plan, Detective. I'll head back to the lab and get this stuff started. I want to know what I'm looking for."

"I'm sure you'll let me know if you find anything?" He couldn't stop himself from asking.

"I was about to ask you the same thing." Her eyes met his, and he felt the undertow of emotion. They had a lot of unfinished business, and none of it had anything to do with work.

Shia dropped her phone back in her pocket and looked up at him as if to say something, stopped and stepped away. "Please keep me posted, Detective. I'll be at headquarters." She leaned over and gathered up her supplies. She flipped up her hood and strode off without looking back.

Ryan watched her leave, feeling the desire to say something, but having no idea what to say. She'd opened his eyes and saved his life, and had done something to his heart in the process. Her world was a place of unexplainable phenomenon; things normal humans couldn't, or wouldn't, see. Wishing it was simple again wasn't going to make it so. He would have an easier time putting the eruption back into a volcano, brick by brick.

Shia faded from the perimeter. Ryan waited a moment; the look in her eyes something he could almost touch.

"O'Sho," he commanded over his shoulder at the patrolman. "Get me a few uniforms. We need to start canvasing the area."

CHAPTER 3

The pace of the snow picked up, and Ryan was oddly grateful. The mixture of frost and snow would ensure any footprints they found in the grounds of Franklin Square would be easier to track.

If there were any.

Two younger patrolmen walked back to where Ryan reviewed details with the veteran O'Shaughnessy. He turned his gaze to the younger men. They cast long shadows in the first light of dawn. "Anything to report, fellas?"

"Nothing, sir," said one of them. The other nodded, pulling his wet cap down on his forehead.

Christ, Ryan thought, these kids are so green they should have flowers. Still, none of the other officers had found anything either. There were no records of aerial transport. The White House auto-cannons hadn't been activated. Two of the law firms had even sent paralegals in to share the video from their cameras. Everything came up blank.

O'Shaughnessy's voice broke Ryan from his funk. "Maybe ol' Abigail Adams decided to do her laundry a few blocks away from home."

Ryan shook his head. O'Sho was referencing the legend of President John Adams' wife haunting their home off of Lafayette Square a few blocks away. "We're really down to ghost stories already?"

The big man shrugged. "It's the best I got, Detective. We've been at this for hours, and there are no fibers, not even a shoe print, or a toe print for that matter, other than his. Maybe his killer popped here out of thin air."

"Think I should cross-reference the airline schedule from Reagan Airport, O'Sho? No," Ryan returned. "We have his footprints, but only his. Either he came here with someone too light to bend a blade of grass, or we have a killer very, very good at covering his trail."

The older cop nodded. "Either way, I'm punching the clock. I'm heading home."

"It's Saturday, right? Kids have a soccer game or yard sale or something like that?"

O'Sho winked. "My kids are in college, out of state, you can bet your ass. I'm heading home for some of that good, old, married white folk monkey business."

Ryan laughed. He slapped the older man on the shoulder. "Get out of here, Pat. I'll see you in church."

Officer O'Shaughnessy laughed louder than Ryan had. "That'll be the day, kid. Good luck with the paperwork."

Ryan watched the older man leave. Patrick was a family man, through and through, the modern day embodiment of the 20th century Irish beat cop. He rubbed his eyes. Second time in two days he caught himself envying the American dream family. The job must be getting to him.

He ordered the younger men to take the evidence to headquarters. The evidence was a few hairs and a plaster cast of a shoe print he already knew would match the vic. As for the killer, they were still staring at a blank page. Once he was left alone beside his beloved cruiser, he reached into his pocket and pulled out his phone. Shia would want a report on what they had, or hadn't, found.

Michelle Adams, Shellie to her sister samurai, stared down at the sleeping child. So innocent in sleep. Sierra Tate. Five years old, newly orphaned, and recently rescued from a nasty Rissu demon. The child hadn't said a word yet. She'd taken a serious cut from the Rissu's claws when she, Taji, and...she glanced at the man slouched in slumber in the chair next to the bed, and Rex rescued her. She'd fallen into a healing state and remained there for days.

Taji had taken one look at the big shifter and promptly declared Shellie in good hands. Then, the little Asian cat disappeared on her, leaving her with a deadly Jaguar. She checked the young one's breathing, happy at least it was steady and strong.

"She should be safe enough for us to move her." She started at the sound of his deep, gravely voice. Every cell in her body went on high alert, as if he purred at her.

"Why would I do that? If I move her, I'm taking her home to my sisters." She scooted around to the other side of the bed, putting it between them both. She knew he wouldn't harm the child. It was herself she was more worried about. He looked at her as if he wanted to pounce her.

"She needs to heal. Let me take you to our clan. We have more resources for you to do your healing. That's what you are, right?" He glanced pointedly at her hands. She looked down, her rings sparked back up at her, gemstones of various kinds glimmering. "We can keep you safe until she's ready to travel further. This chalet is too unprotected."

"Why would I trust you? I can take care of myself." She murmured. It was true. Sierra needed time and space to heal. She would be better off with her sisters around her, perhaps even heal faster. She'd only packed her rudimentary healing kit, enough for herself. She needed to scout the mountains for more remedies, but couldn't leave the child unprotected in the Chalet. He had helped her dispatch the Rissu with deadly claws of his own. She'd never seen a full sized jaguar.

She bit her lip and took a deep breath. Think, she needed to think. She couldn't with him staring at her. Long black hair curled down around the hard angles of his face. Dark eyes shimmered in the low light of the chalet. A hint of facial hair graced his jawline. In all black as he was, he'd likely scare Sierra to death if she chose to open her eyes right then.

"Our healer moved to another clan. We have her entire space and supplies you can use."

She cut a look at him. "You're trying to bribe me now?"

"Anything I can to get you both to a safe place. I can't defend you here while you try to heal her." He answered.

"You came out of nowhere." Shellie twisted one of her rings around on a finger. "Taji seems to think you won't harm us."

"Healer, what I saw the two of you just do with swords. I'd say I might be the one who should be worried." He smiled, his teeth a slash of white against the tan skin.

"No harm will come to the child or myself. And when I deem we're ready to depart..."

"I'll make sure you find safe passage home. Even if I have to escort you myself." He promised.

Shellie sat down on the bed next to Sierra. "We can leave at dawn, unless there are any changes, she should be safe to move."

"Good, then rest. I'll do a perimeter sweep and be right outside the door if you need me." He stood. Shellie drew back somewhat, startled again by how tall and large he was. The room shrunk with his presence.

His gaze darkened for a moment and then smoothed out. He looked as if he wanted to say something more, but decided against it, simply bowing to her slightly before striding out of the room and out of the chalet.

She breathed a sigh of relief before collapsing next to Sierra's small form on the bed. She hadn't let on how exhausted she was, nor that she needed to heal. She needed to stay awake, keep watch, but her body took over sending her tumbling down into the healing realms of a samurai sleep.

Rex Kade forced himself to calm down, taking deep, full breaths of the cold mountain air. The little redheaded healer had him in knots since he'd picked up her scent on the outer edge of their territory. He'd have to thank Dane, their pack leader, for sending him out.

When he'd seen the demon dog take a swipe at her, he'd gone into a full fledge killing rage, shifting without thought and jumping into the fray. She and her sister had been poetry in motion hacking at the demon until he'd moved away from the child. He still wasn't sure who'd made the killing blow, one of their blades or his claws.

He'd thought they be frightened by his appearance. Neither batted an eye, the young Asian one simply declared him safe, then shifted into a small mountain lion and bounded away.

An energy shift from inside the chalet rippled over him. He raced back in, ready to defend the healer and her charge. Instead, he found her face first on the bed. He approached cautiously. His eyes darted everywhere, taking everything in. Nothing out of place other than her gorgeous body planted on top of the comforter. He started when the cell phone next to the bed chirped to life. He glanced at the screen, the smart phone flashed at him.

The words "Answer me, Jaguar," flashed on the screen. With a bit of trepidation, he swiped his thumb across it and lifted it to his ear.

"Mr. Kade," a woman's voice came over the line. "Jace informs me Shellie's bio-rhythms have dropped her into a healing sleep and the young one next to her is in the same state."

"Who is this?" And, more importantly, how the hell did she know his name.

"Dr. Shia Ronin. I am Shellie's sister." She answered. "I need you to open the backpack that Taji left in the living room. There should be at least two syringes in there, one for Shellie. Use only a quarter of the other on the child. Will you be moving them to safer ground, or do I need to have Taji return to bring them home?"

Rex strode back into the living room and quickly located the backpack. Sure enough, two syringes filled with blue liquid lay wrapped in a black leather cloth.

"I was going to wait till morning as she'd asked me. Now, I'll have them moved to safety within the hour." He frowned. "How did you know...?"

Laughter came over the line. "I know a lot more than most of the world at large, Shifter. Take care of my sister and our new charge. It will be nice to meet your clan when they're ready."

The phone went dead in his hand. He shook his head and dropped the device in his front shirt pocket. He'd deal with the security breach when he had the females safely protected with his clan. He pulled his own phone out of his back pocket and hit a number.

When the voice on the other end answered, he commanded. "Lock on to my signal, I need transport for two wounded and myself within the hour. Come silent." And he clicked it off.

He stared at the syringe for a moment before sitting down on the bed. It dipped with his weight. He gently turned Shellie over on her back. Worry tugged deep in his stomach when she didn't even flinch under his touch. She'd been skittish since he'd broken in on their fight with the dog-like demon. He checked her breathing and her heart rate, both slow but strong. With as much care as he could, he set the needle into her skin, injecting what he could only hope was a medicine. When her condition showed no worse for it, he moved over to the sleeping child and did exactly as Dr. Ronin asked.

And then he sat down to wait.

CHAPTER 4

Ryan pulled off a glove and prepared to dial when the phone vibrated in his hand. A few seconds later, the incoming number filled the screen.

"Oh, man, I don't need this right now." He stared at it a few seconds longer, shame spreading up his spine with every unanswered ring. He gave in and tapped the call button. "Calder."

"Hello, Mijo. I'm surprised you're up this early."

"Still up from last night, Padre, on a murder scene." Ryan clenched his teeth. He sounded cold and bitter. Father Francisco Munoz deserved better. He'd always been patient and compassionate with Ryan, and he'd been one of the few others to survive an encounter with demon. His Faith had never faltered. He was a good man. Maybe he'd intercepted Ryan's wishful thinking about a normal life, and he was going to sweep in with some brochure and heavenly sales pitch.

"I will pray for those who have suffered this night, as I do each day."

"This one might need a little extra, something like a Super Size prayer if you got one."

Father Munoz exhaled slowly. "You are wondering why I called, Mijo."

"I would be lying if I said otherwise, Padre. How can I help you?"

"I'm not calling on my behalf. I am calling to extend an invitation to you from the children of our congregation." Ouch. Ryan had set up a foundation years ago, and the children in Father Munoz's parish were the ones who benefitted. Ryan had yet to attend an event and to do anything other than completely cause distraction, embarrassment, and the occasional civil suit.

"I don't know if this is the best time, Padre."

"If you would prefer, I can call back, and you can pretend you didn't get my call, and I will find a lesson to share with the children."

Ryan pulled his head from the phone and rested it on the cold roof of the Impala. After a pause, he pulled the phone back to his ear. "I'm listening."

Father Munoz's tone changed in an instant. "Excellent, Mijo. The children want me to invite you to the Winter Celebration Festival. There will be a play, with music, crafts, and activities."

"Did you just invite me to a kids' party, Padre?"

The priest laughed. "I did, Mijo, and the children have insisted you also invite the lovely Dr. Ronin as your guest."

"What?!"

"She was a delight at the foundation gala, in your absence. She was also present when they were frightened from the courtyard by that evil being. The children want to thank her. They have been rehearsing very hard. I know she will be delighted by their performance."

Ryan stared at his reflection in the driver's window of the Impala. His face was equal parts confusion and anger. Part of him swore that Father Munoz must have worked in used cars or real estate before he'd found God.

"I, I owe her a call. I'll see what she says." He slapped

his hand to his forehead the moment the words left his mouth.

Father Munoz enthusiasm practically set the phone alight with holy fire. "Excellent, Mijo. I will inform the children of your decision."

Ryan stammered. "Wait! What?"

"Peace be with you, Mijo," Father Munoz stated, and the line went dead.

Ryan stared at the phone for so long he couldn't measure it. Snow fell and melted on the screen, on his bare skin, and on the cruiser.

"Detective."

Ryan pulled himself back to the moment at the sound of another voice. He looked around, but was still alone.

"Detective."

"Yes, Jace?"

"Lady Ronin requires an update. Shall we contact her now?"

Ryan stared at the Impala. He loved his car. He really loved his car. Now that the AI had improved it, he was a little less certain of how much he adored the cruiser. "Start up. Heated seats. Interior at 77. I can't feel my face. Make it 78. Once we're on 18th, place the call."

He slipped into the familiar comfort of the driver's seat and stared blankly through the windshield. "A children's party? What the hell?"

She glared at the slides under the microscope. She should have set Jace to this task, not like she hadn't programmed him to manage all of it. Yet, for some reason, she refused to give up the hands-on management of some things, like working on the postmortem blood and fluid analysis.

"Lady Ronin?" The electronic voice echoed in the lab.

Good thing she'd locked all the doors when she'd come in. "Yes, Jace?"

"Why don't you let me do the analysis, and you can focus on where you really want to focus? Based on the heat signatures I sent you, we should be researching those as well."

Shia didn't bother to respond. She should have taken the evidence to her home lab, as something on the edge of her senses had her worried that this kill was blatantly otherworldly. Although, she had a state-of-the-art lab, nothing but the best for the Washington PD Metro, she needed more. She should offer an anonymous grant to add in more of the items she and Jace created in recent years.

Honestly, she should setup a dummy corporation and sell the tech. It would be one more way to fund their Samurai House.

She sighed and leaned back on the medical stool. The AI was correct. Her back protested the shift. She'd been hunched over analyzing the blood for what had to have been hours. She stretched.

"Fine, you take over the analysis. Load the crime scene photos into the system and start running a scenario of exactly how this boy had his head ripped off." For the life of her, she'd never seen something like it. It screamed demon even though she hadn't sensed anything on scene. If it was a demon, how many had she missed in the past?

She should check in with Ryan. She shook her head at herself. Detective Calder. He was Detective Calder. He had to remain Detective Calder. She didn't need to be on a first name basis with him. If their last encounter proved anything, it proved she was slipping and had some major clean up to do.

She tapped her fingers on the counter before her, but it would help to know if he'd found anything else on scene. Although, she wouldn't be surprised if the answer came back no.

This one was smart.

"And Jace?"

"Yes, Lady Ronin?"

"Run a mock profit and loss statement on selling the tech you and I have been creating to analyze crime scene data. The stuff the human forces can use. Include all relevant expenses such as corporation set up and manufacturing. I'm sure you can run multiple scenarios at once." She turned and flipped open her personal laptop.

"Of course, m'lady."

She would swear the AI's voice banks lit up with the idea of selling their tech, more so than the crime scene analysis itself. The screen opened up before her as she started searching through the demonology database the Samurai House maintained. She had thousands of years to sift through, even with the automatic search features.

She'd started the journals by hand, eventually having those who came into being behind her do the same. When technology started to advance, they'd each painstakingly began to move their work digital. In the last fifteen years or so, everything had become 1's and 0's and now, the database of the largest chronicles of demonology stored thousands of terabytes of data on demons behind several locked down firewalls. Only the sisters could get to it.

She'd made sure of that.

If the world had even the barest hint of the Others who walked among their kind, chaos, hysteria, panic would ensue. Those who preyed on the criminal. Those who stayed under the radar. Those who didn't set out to cause mass hysteria and destruction. Those, she let walk. It helped keep the balance. She'd finally understood the laws of checks and balances several hundreds of years into her being. There needed to be a balance. She was required to go after the darker side, the purely evil side.

Over seven hundred hits showed up in her search pattern.

"Naraku." She uttered the soft Japanese curse under her breath. Well, no one said it was going to be easy, and it sure beat the hell out of combing through the hand written journals Ilsa had stored in their Norway headquarters. Especially when Aureline, her South American sister, and Iniko, her African sister, both had such horrible handwriting. She'd made them translate their own files.

"I heard that." The AI voice commented.

"Wasn't keeping it a secret." Shia sighed as she started speed-reading the listings. "John Milton had nothing on our journals. But the man had a knack for getting very close to the truth on so many of these things."

"You think he could see them?" Jace asked.

Shia continued to read. "I'm pretty sure he had to have been able to see something. Or at least, something enough to start asking around and researching."

Her phone vibrated across the lab counter. She cast a glance at it.

"Are you going to answer that?" Jace asked.

She stared down at Ryan's number knowing she needed to answer it and yet, at the same time dreading it.

"Put him on speaker." She said to Jace instead.

"Dr. Ronin." She stared back at her laptop screen, not really seeing it. "You have news, Detective?"

The engine roared in the background. "Yes, and no, as it stands. You busy?"

Shia half smiled to herself. "I am never not busy, Detective. I have scenarios running, analysis being done, and research going. You?"

"I think I can feel my face again. First time in hours. Nothing like searching for a murderer who isn't in the mood to be found. You want hypotheticals or the evidentiary findings so far?"

Shia frowned. If there were no other signs of the demon, she was in far more trouble than she thought. She glared at the seven hundred plus hits on her search. She was only on link twenty-two. At this rate, she'd be up for a week. Jace stayed wisely silent, for once.

"Both." She said. The more data she had in her head, in the file, the better.

"Let's go with the facts first," he replied in the tone that indicated he was practicing his particular style of aggressive driving. "We found foot prints and DNA. That's the good news. The bad news is they're both going to match our vic. There's no second set of prints, no video coverage, nothing tangible if you know what I mean."

Shia sighed. "Only the energy signatures no one else is going to recognize."

She continued to scan the journals.

"Did the energy foot print touch down anywhere else? Were you using that as well?" She asked.

"How exactly am I supposed to do that? I used over a dozen beat cops with flashlights, IR scanners, UV and darklight detectors, but we got nothing. Unless you suddenly go into business selling your tech from the future, I can't scan for stuff like that in the line of duty."

Shia looked over at her phone, eyes wide. "Ahh, Detective, I gave you the lead with your phone and the mapping software. Or better yet, Jace did all on his own. You didn't use it?"

"Okay, if you're going to do that, you're going to need to land me an acting coach. When I suddenly grab a patrol and yell, 'he went that way', I'm going to need a reason. Otherwise, the DA is gonna say I used my gut, and he'll never prosecute. My justice isn't your justice, doc."

Did he just suggest she go corporate with her tech? Was the man a mind reader?

"I don't care whether you can use it for making your case. I need it for tracking mine. Get creative. I do it all the time. You never batted an eyelash at it in the past."

"If you mean the couple of times I had a Red Lobster mascot with rabies attacking me, I get your logic. This isn't one of those times. Give me something to work with, Shi...Dr. Ronin. I need a starting point."

Shia stopped herself. He really didn't see the full picture yet. The times she'd changed things, made them fit the mold, made them suit. He was seeing things now; he hadn't connected the past cases yet. In her world, he was a newborn still learning his senses. She bit her lip. "I can't give you that yet, Detective. I'm still trying to find the answers myself."

She continued to scan the journals. As much as she'd rather listen to the sound of his voice, even over the speakers in the lab, she needed to remain focused. This anomaly would wreck too much havoc if she couldn't concentrate.

There was a long pause on the line before Ryan spoke again. "I appreciate that. Fingerprints and DNA are already being processed. If the vic had a record, I'll have something for you ASAP. If he flew below the radar like this attacker, things will take a bit longer." He sounded like he had more to say, but the engine was the only noise from his end of the line.

"I understand, Detective." She did, only too well. She started when her phone beeped at her. Raisa's image flashed across the smart phone. She hesitated.

"Ok, we both sound chillier than a vodka bar in Kiev.

Let me toss something out at you as an icebreaker, that okay?"

"I'd like that Detective, but I have an incoming call I need to take. Emergency. You have anything more?" She asked.

"Yeah, my Chief Sergeant filled my head with an image of his overweight ass and his pasty white wife making the most of their empty nest. You got any magic potion to scrub away every mental image a person..." He stopped in mid-sentence, reacting to something else. "Damn it. I have to take this call. I'll contact you with the scan results."

She hit End on the call with Ryan. "Jace, I'm going home. Continue analysis." She flipped the laptop closed and picked up her phone. "Thanks for calling me back so quickly." She said as she held it up to her ear. "I need you to do something for me."

Ryan watched the early December snow flurries chase each other across the slowly darkening sky. The headlights of the Impala caught the extremes of their back and forth patterns in the wind. He was exhausted, fighting the theories of his latest case with resolving unsolved issues from the past. He had spent hours in the frosty grass, only to confirm that Shia Ronin was correct. Their opponent was something supernatural, and nothing he could stop on his own.

When he finally reached out to admit his own limitation, she was already far ahead of him, as usual. He felt confused, small, powerless until he focused once again on the victim. Demons, faeries, unicorns, vampires be damned, he had a case to solve, and he was going to pull in the right resources at the right time, samurai medical examiner included.

"Ryan? Oh my God, I can't believe you picked up. Can you talk? Just a minute? Maybe a couple minutes? I really need to hear the sound of your voice. Are you okay? Is everything okay? Are you somewhere nearby we could talk? You know, just to talk. We don't ever get to talk anymore."

Ryan squeezed his eyes shut. He recognized the voice as soon as she had mentioned his name. He inhaled but couldn't breathe out. Her torment felt like a fist struck against his chest. Gritting his teeth, he blew out a breath and hardly managed to whisper her name. "Felicia."

FBI Special Agent Felicia Simone responded like a loyal dog. "Yes, yes, Ryan. Your voice makes me so happy. Say my name again, so I can hear it clearly. No, wait, I should record this. This is important. I should record this."

Ryan slammed his fist against the dashboard. Felicia had been exposed to forces beyond her understanding and had suffered as a result. He couldn't explain what had happened. She wouldn't understand, and she would be the next target for mainstream media looking for a government agent to humiliate.

He and Felicia had loved one another once, in a place and time that demanded a love born of desperation. He wouldn't hang her out to dry. He couldn't, but now he had no idea what other route to take. She was broken, and it was all his fault.

"Ryan?" Felicia asked, splitting through the haze of his desperation.

He fumbled on the word but finally asked, "Yes?"

"I have a call coming in. I'll call you back as soon as I can. Thanks for listening."

Ryan started, stopped, started again and finally recognized the dead call screen in his hand. He downshifted and parked by the side of the road, finding his hazard lights in the process. The "Call Ended" screen met his gaze, flanked by the turn signals. For all his experience behind the wheel, Ryan couldn't bring himself to lift a finger.

Tourists and commuters passed by the Impala parked on the shoulder. Some slowed down assuming the local police radar trap. Others shifted lanes, believing urban legends about plate scanning. Life in suburban DC went on as usual, save the soul of one dedicated cop and those on the other end of his call.

CHAPTER 5

Raisa Aleski closed her eyes and took a few deep breaths. It took time to work the energy patterns into those she wanted to achieve. If anyone else had asked her to do what she was about to do, she would have said no, but Shia called in a favor. She owed the First.

Da, it was her duty. Who was she kidding? As much as she liked to be a bitch about it all, when one of her sisters called and requested her unique talents, she dropped everything and went. She added some attitude to it, a little more attitude for some rather than others. If Ilsa called, she took her time in answering; something about the blonde Scandinavian set her off. But Shia, her quiet, calm, countenance...her being her, the First, the one who'd found her. It made it all different.

She needed the break anyway. The crazy stunt driver on set of her latest gig was driving her insane. She muttered an old Russian curse under her breath. She did not need him creeping into her job or her mind. She forced all thoughts of the gorgeous, but crazy Kyrin out.

Eyes opened as engines roared above her. She took the last puff on the cigarette she had in hand and then threw it to the ground, crushing it underfoot. Been there, done that, bad for her, except it wasn't going to kill her anyways. She'd take the vice. She'd done far worse in her time. She was about to do far worse. She pulled a picture out of her pocket, memorized the details of the man staring back at her. With a quick flip of her hair, she tilted her head back and pulled the energy around her. It pulsed, shivered and in a moment, stabilized again. She glanced down at her hands. No change.

She turned and looked into the window beside her.

Rather than her normal redheaded razor cut, the man's visage from the photo stared back. She, he, flashed a quick smile. She reached down, straightened her imaginary jacket, grabbed the large leather duffle bag at her feet and strode off across the airport tarmac.

Show time.

A little over two hours later, the left engine sputtered two miles from her target. Located in the Exuma Cays, Bahamas, the island sparkled like all the others nestled around it. Any other time she would have loved to steal some time to take a dip in the Caribbean waters. The white sands and clear waters of the private island would call out to even the most hard-hearted person. She might be jaded, but she wasn't stupid.

And, she was crashing.

Instead of panicking, Raisa's gloved fingers flipped the correct switches in the proper sequence, following all the rules and regulations, as any skilled pilot would do. Her heartbeat in excitement as the nose drifted down. Seconds behind the left, the right engine died. Lights on the panels before her began to light up, beep. She smiled and took off the headset. No control tower voices to guide her in, no one to check in with. She knew, if anyone could see her, her eyes would be glowing with the unholy light of delight.

This was what she lived for. The rush, the acceleration of her heart beat, the power that flowed through her.

She snapped the energies around her and blinked out seconds before impact. Every bone in her body would have shattered if she'd been in the small twin engine when it hit the ocean waves.

Instead, she let the energy waves carry her right back to the one person she needed to check in with even though she'd rather hunt down her crazy stunt driver and work off the adrenaline rush she'd caused herself.

Some days, it was good to be immortal.

Shia stared at the flat panels before her. So many more than she'd had in the lab. She loved her home office. State of the art and completely secure. Governments around the world would kill for the network she and her sisters ran.

Some tried. All failed. She'd made sure of it.

Jace streamed crime scene data on several screens. The journal archives ran searches on several others. On two others, she watched the scenarios Jace pulled together on what had happened to the teenage boy in the park. People thought she couldn't multi-task.

She shifted in the large leather chair, tilting her head, her long dark hair falling down over her shoulder. She flipped it back as she watched the recreation of how exactly the boy's head could have been ripped off. The force had to have come from inside him for the exact process of his head being so removed from his jaw and neck. Every other scenario she'd had Jace build her was off each time. It didn't matter the weapon, none of them matched the exact torque and twist. It had to have come from inside him.

So much for the dojo theory.

What the kind of demon could have come from inside him? And how had it gotten into him in the first place?

She switched screens and started to pay closer attention to the crime scene photos. Tall and skinny, the kid barely had any mass to him at all. A few tattoos, standard variety, here and there. She wondered who'd allowed him to get the markings. She'd bet he wasn't old enough to have passed the legal age limit for them. Then again, with the right credentials or even the wrong ones, people could get a variety of things done.

Nothing cried out at her. Naraku. Too easy, she knew it.

She twisted again and started tapping out commands on the keyboard, alternating her searches through the demon database.

"Jace, leave a message for Detective Calder. I need to ask him a few questions when he has a moment." She said.

"Any reason you don't want to call him yourself?" He asked.

She cut a glance to the time on her screen. "It's 5am. I'm pretty sure he still has a need to sleep. It's not life threatening. At least, so long as a new victim doesn't show up tonight. Leave the message so he gets it when he gets up."

She brought one knee up to her chest and leaned against it. Demons. Every time they tried to get more creative, and every time she thought she'd made headway on understanding how things worked in her universe, the rules shifted. At least it kept them all from getting bored, even if she would like a brief break from the insanity.

She clicked the screens off. She needed to take time for herself. A quick shower, some food. Some time not staring at the screens, maybe her brain would engage again. She had to know this type of demon. With their extensive studies and training, there were very few things in the Otherworld she hadn't run across and done battle with a time or two.

"Keep running the scenarios and scans. I'm taking a quick break." She padded on bare feet across the warehouse floor. The cold concrete didn't even cause her to flinch. A quick sprint up the open wooden staircase and she reached the second floor she'd built into the space. Open and airy, she'd kept most of the top floor for herself, a haven, her retreat. A place she could come home to and relax. A separate section, she'd designed for her sisters, stood apart from her own.

Rice paper walls, hard wood floors, and the more traditional Japanese furniture she'd had through the years. She'd tried out other models of living, but finally returned to the simple, more Zen like method. She also had an AI who liked to decorate apparently. She wasn't sure how the warehouse had been renovated so well while she'd been gone. She was happy it had.

She smiled when she reached the bathroom. Jace already cranked up the shower so the room was steaming and warm. He was almost as good as having a man around. Of course, there were those days she missed a warm male body to snuggle up with.

The voice system in the Impala and his phone vibrated at the same time. Ryan tapped the button on the steering wheel, answering the call after one ring. "Calder."

"Detective." Jace answered.

"Jace?" Ryan looked at his dashboard.

"She's in the shower." He said.

Ryan's gaze shifted from the dashboard to his phone, back to his dashboard. "Jace, did you just call my car?"

"No, well, yes..." If an AI could sigh, Ryan would

swear he did. "She asked me to place a call to you. I did so."

"You called my car."

"Technically, she called you. Regardless sir, she's requesting an update."

"She didn't call me from the shower, Jace. You called me. Admit it. You called my car...from my car."

"No sir...I called you from her phone, in the warehouse. Just because I also have access in your car does not mean I initiated the call from your car to you. I did exactly as she asked."

"You called me from her phone to make it look like she was calling me. You could have opened your mouth and said something directly." Ryan chuckled, picturing C-3PO on the high school debate team. "You are a sucker for protocol, Jace."

"I am not above safe guarding my tracks, sir. She can delete me."

"Can't even admit you lost an argument to a sleep-deprived homicide detective who only started this conversation to avoid the distraction of your boss in the shower? You're slipping, Jace. How 'bout we let this game go and you take me to her?"

"My point exactly, sir. GPS coordinates are on screen. Try not to scare the locals. It will irritate her. I will open the garage bay."

Ryan rubbed his eyes. Without the mental chess game with Jace, he had very little to keep his mind from picturing Shia's lithe body beneath steaming water. He took a slug of ice-cold coffee, the taste making him shake his head. "Lead the way, Jace. Might as well deliver the bad news in person."

Jace waited until the Detective's car turned the corner, then opened the garage doors to the warehouse. The Impala entered the garage. Ryan slapped his palms against the steering wheel. This wasn't her place, at least not the place she called her own when he'd last visited. The moment the car reached its destination, he killed the engine and opened the driver's door. It wasn't likely, but it was possible Jace had been hacked, and he was walking into a trap.

Ryan moved quickly through the ground floor, noting no signs of life, serene, sterile. He held his pistol in one hand, his flashlight in the other. Recognizing nothing more than flashing screens in what he assumed was an office, he found the stairs, ascending them slowly. The upstairs decor was different. It was all rice paper and wood flooring. He heard a sudden movement at the far end of the flat and advanced, crossing and aiming both his flashlight and 9mm.

Ryan's light hit nothing but steam, and he barked to take control. "Don't move!"

The slender form in front of him stopped in mid-movement and with a simple pivot snagged the sword from the bed. He realized by the movement, the figure before him was female. She turned with the towel still snarled in her hair, her skintight yoga pants swooshing her move. Her upper body, bare. Sword upraised, palm out, she dropped into a very low cat stance.

Ryan swallowed. Hard. The body of Shia Ronin appeared an arm's length away from him. Ryan took a step back on instinct, then moved his eyes over her form, and back to the sword in her hand. One moment, he was thankful to be alive. The next, he was praying for a photographic memory. When he realized she wasn't going to behead him, he lowered his gun. "Whoa, Shia. Truce?"

"Stars above, Jace." She snapped. She ripped her sword hand out and around drawing the towel out of her hair and around her chest. Apparently, her making the Detective forget the warehouse hadn't stuck.

She glared at him, sword in hand and towel wrapped around her chest. "Give me one good reason, Detective. You are in my home, without my leave or request. Be very, very glad I didn't sever your head from your shoulders."

Ryan ran a hand through his hair as he re-holstered his gun. "You called me, Shia."

"No, I had Jace issue a call thinking you'd be asleep. Not show up at my home." She stopped.

"Jace?" She flipped her sword up, collapsed it, and laid it on the bed.

"Yes, m'lady?" The AI asked.

"You are about one minute from me rewiring your circuits." She knew exactly how Ryan ended up her home. She wasn't stupid. The AI would get a lesson in who had built whom.

"Okay," Ryan started, "he messed up. I was up. I am still up from our murder scene. How bout we reign it in, have a cup of tea, and we focus on the case? I'd hate for you to kill your AI or me."

She tilted her wet head at him. He, who was in her bedroom of all places and trying to be reasonable. "Kitchen. Now. I'll be there in a minute. Maybe, just maybe I won't change his circuits."

She turned her back, her naked back, expecting him to leave.

Ryan focused on her back. He swallowed at the

sight of the exquisitely etched cherry blossom branch and kanji characters down her right shoulder blade and back. The pale pink blossoms shimmered on her skin. He wanted her. He had wanted her from the first time he had seen her. He'd dreamt of her. And there she was, a few feet away. He paused and closed his eyes. She was right for him. He was right for her.

"Damn it all, man," he told himself. "Make your move."

An image of fire flashed across his vision. He looked at his hand and watched as fire crept along his fingertips, drove along his knuckles and then engulfed both of his hands. He screamed a soundless noise as the flames accelerated up his arms and covered his entire body in seconds. He fanned in earnest at the spreading fire.

Flames closed in from all sides. He suddenly had tunnel vision, but the periphery was enclosed in white light, not darkness. His skin felt dry and tight, like he'd woken up with a sunburn. The temperature rose from there. He blindly slapped at his neck and shoulders, assured he was burning. His skin melted on his bones.

The fire seared his eyes. He felt them boiling. Colors evaporated, leaving only shades of white flame and gray ashes. He clenched his teeth against the pain. He wanted to breathe, but every inhale filled his lungs with fire. He couldn't define if he was burning from the outside in or the inside out. The flames engulfed him. Every cell erupted.

From outside his body, he felt himself backing away from the fiery agony he couldn't define. Still staring at Shia, he stopped, turned, and headed down the stairs to the kitchen. He took the stairs two or three at a time. He struck the wall once with his shoulder, or so he imagined. He reached the kitchen sink and cranked the cold water. The liquid flow was a different type of burn on his skin. The icy water quickly dispelled the feeling of fire on his skin. He leaned on both elbows against the sink. The temperature change made him dizzy. His legs were suddenly useless. He leaned over the sink, the combination of water and sweat making a steady drip on the stainless steel.

After an eternity of fire in his lungs, he was able to steady his breathing. He opened his eyes. The room was dark, and he saw a myriad of white silhouettes. He closed his eyes again, waiting for the after images to fade. He doused his head once more. When he opened his eyes once more, he made out small changes in texture among the darkness. He wasn't burning. He wasn't frozen. He was back in charge.

Ryan grabbed a glass off of the counter, intent on pouring a cool glass of water. The glass slipped from his grip and teetered at the edge of counter. He reached to save it and missed. The glass shattered on the floor with an audible crash. He slammed his palms down on the counter top and then stomped on what was left of the glass. He kicked several times until the rage inside of him subsided, and the glass was no longer any semblance of a target.

She laid the sword on her bed, slowly, methodically, with great care. Her breathing even and slow, as much as it wanted to outpace her.

Ryan in her bedroom.

Her heart hit triple time before she could contain it. No. She snagged her sword sheaths, dropped them both in their places before she pulled the shirt over her body. Damn it. She'd wanted to leave her weapons in their resting places. Instead, she had one well-armed Detective in her midst, in her home. She left the towel on the floor, certain the bots Jace built would remove them and headed to the kitchen.

As she strode into the kitchen, Ryan answered her before she could ask over the lip of his steaming coffee mug. She may have hid her body from his view, but she apparently couldn't keep him from her microwave. "Truth be told, my GPS led me here."

She glared at him. "I'm not listed."

"Not in the current yellow pages, but the ones from the future have you as a prime crime fighting destination. You own a regular 22nd century Batcave."

The air at the other end of the kitchen island shimmered, and then warped, and twisted. A new form appeared at the end of the long island bar. Red headed, wickedly hard, lean body wrapped in skin tight jeans and gray concert T-Shirt boasting the dark outline of the band Nine Inch Nails. Her smile looked lethal to anyone in her path with sharp, pearl white canines nipping her at her full lips. "Interrupting, am I?"

Shia's hand landed hard and loud on the wooden counter. "You all." She stopped and took a deep breath. "Raisa. Report. Jace, record."

The redhead glanced at Shia, her moss green eyes narrowed, and then cut the tall, sexy human a glance with all feigned innocent and curiosity. "All taken care of, da. Wanted to let you know before I return to my space."

Ryan fought his instincts and stopped. His fingers gripped the pistol, but he didn't draw. He exhaled, set his feet in case he needed to defend himself, and observed. He didn't need a formal introduction. The ability to bend time and distance was enough. He knew another of Shia's sisters had magically appeared. As they spoke,

Ryan tried to make sense of it. Shia's voice mixed with her sister's. They clashed like two notes that wouldn't resolve. He squeezed his eyes shut and ran a hand across his forehead. Each sister may have the voice of an angel, but pulled between them, all he could do was hold on to his own definition of reality.

"This one is..." Raisa angled her head and looked Ryan over. "Hmmm, you play with him, no?" A wicked grin swept over her face. "If not, I'm game."

She trailed a glance over his body.

Shia growled low in her throat. The redhead winked at him and then winked out of her kitchen.

Shia sighed and closed her eyes. Her fingernails curled into the counter space. Could her day get much worse? Dead body, demon attacker, Jace leading one hot, sexy detective back to her doorstep, one sister samurai winking in and out. All she needed was for Ilsa and crew to show up and take up residence.

She opened her eyes and stared over at Ryan. She could see the faint hint of pain and discord ripple across the tight lines in his face as he dropped his hand from the side of his face.

"She's gone, Detective." Shia whispered. "I'm sorry for that. You should not be here. The pounding will go away in a few seconds."

She knew he was experiencing the energy overlap. It couldn't be helped.

Ryan opened his eyes, blinking several times as the pain slowly subsided. He stabilized his breathing. "How 'bout I tell you what my team found in Franklin Square," he muttered through gritted teeth, "And you can explain the impromptu family reunion later?"

"Sounds good to me, Detective. Jace, tea please." She didn't blink when the stove flipped on and the kettle atop it started to warm.

She took a seat at the kitchen island, her hands folded in front of her and stared at him, waiting.

Ryan squeezed his eyes shut again, still trying to clear the fog. "Is this something you get used to in weeks, years, or centuries?"

"It clears. Your body and mind seem to be adapting to the dimensional energies rather rapidly. Raisa can be a little difficult to handle since she can also bend those energies on her own." She glanced over him. "Usually, you have to die first to even see the dimensional energies."

He opened one eye and looked at her. "You realize, if we ever mess things up and go separate ways, I'm going to wind up in a straight-jacket."

She lifted a brow. "I can take those memories away, Detective. It's nothing for me to do. You can go right back to being who and what you were. I'm not sure why you started seeing them in the first place, so I'm not sure how long the ... retention would last." She propped an elbow on the counter and rested her chin in her upturned hand. Her other hand reached out to draw ancient patterns on the marble.

He opened his other eye, exhaled and leaned closer. "If that means forgetting what I've learned about you, forget it. I'll suffer whatever I have to. Besides, what's a little supernatural migraine? I'll lace up my boots and soldier on."

"Honestly, I'm not sure how long it would last." Her eyes lit up at his words and quickly darkened again. Obviously, it hadn't worked for something as simple as forgetting her sanctuary. "You started seeing things on your own. You're not a victim. Victims of attacks, those memories I can take away and even restructure when need be. Those effects have been lasting."

He stopped. "Wait, what? You can make people, victims, forget everything they've seen?"

"Yes. Or restructure what they think they saw. It comes with the job." She stopped tracing the ruins on the counter and tilted her head at him. "Why?"

He frowned, thinking how to form the request that had been boiling in his mind for days. "Would you do that for me? Would you make someone forget?"

"I could," she replied, tilting her head.

"Just me?"

"Of course not. I have had this power for centuries."

Ryan stood. "I need you to use that power."

Shia eyed him, "What are you asking me, Detective?"

"I need you to make someone forget what she saw, what she suffered."

CHAPTER 6

Shia slid open the rice paper doors leading in the lab she'd created on the main floor of the warehouse. She smiled at the startled breath from behind her. She was going to have hell to pay when he realized he'd seen it all before. "Yes, state of the art, better than the prescient has and entirely tapped into the Metro PD system without a trace."

"Just Metro? I don't quite believe that."

She slanted him a look as she gestured to one of the office chairs in front of the large computer consoles. "Our evidence is at Metro PD, Detective."

Ryan sat, his eyes moving all over the lab, taking it all in. He rubbed the base of his neck. This all seemed so familiar.

"Most of it is computer based, so you're not going to find me doing autopsies here." She dropped into her own chair and tapped a few commands out on the keyboard when it flipped over to reveal itself on the desk. A similar one opened in front of Ryan. "I actually don't need to perform them in person anymore. Jace and I have been working on several new methods of seeing into the body in minute detail without cutting it open."

Images began appearing on screen.

"3D printing and modeling. That's pretty damn impressive. Of course, someone beat you to it with the initial vic. I don't get the 'how', though. This wasn't even like gutting a deer. It was more like the reverse."

"Jace, show the video." Shia pointed up at the screen as the vid started in slow motion. "We've determined the only possible way for Tyler Daniels head to have been removed in the manner it was, was if the initial force had come from within him."

Ryan turned from the screen to Shia. "When I was on duty, on patrol, in Fallujah, I saw a kid jump on a grenade to save his unit. The shrapnel tore through a dozen organs. It was chaotic. It was nothing like this, nothing so focused. What the hell kind of force are we talking about?"

Her eyes widened, "This is nothing so disparate. We're looking for a centralized force coming up and through his body." She marked the trail with her finger. "The energy source seemed to be hovering here. And then ripped upward, see the orange lines?"

She continued. "Physical enough in the sense that it can affect things here. But no, the killer in this instance is not human." She frowned at the screen and photos of all distinguishing marks began to appear on the screen. "I've been studying every mark, mole, tattoo, and skin irritation to see if I can figure out what kind of creature could do this. Jace is still searching the demonology database as well."

"And, now, I have to figure out how to make this one appear..." She sighed. "Self-inflicted."

Ryan stared at the screen, one fist raised before his mouth. "Self..." he stopped, frowning and staring back at the monitors. "Hey, the girl, your sister..."

She turned her head, her dark hair falling in her eyes

and tucked it back behind her ears before it could irritate her further. "Raisa?"

"Yeah, her. Are there other things that can do what she does?"

"What do you mean, Detective?"

Ryan smirked. "I don't mean get under your skin by hitting on me. I'm sure she has the market cornered on that. I mean, the thing she did, where she popped in here and out again with just a thought."

Shia narrowed her eyes at him. "Raisa hits on any male within her sight. And are you suggesting one of my sisters would be capable of exploding a human from the inside out?"

"No," he shook his head and stood. "I'm not saying it was one of you. That's why I asked if there was something else that could do it. Has it ever happened? Has something, a whatever, ever popped in a space already occupied?"

The tension in her shoulders eased. Some. "That's what I have Jace researching. We're comparing all the identifying marks on his body with every known demon attack any of us has faced. Raisa can only bend, if bend is even the correct term, bend energy for herself or someone she is immediately touching. This demon, had to have been called. There are no open portals, or we'd be inundated with them."

Ryan paced, as he often did while going over a case. "Called. Summoned, right? Doesn't a summoning take blood and talismans and a ceremony or something? Go slow with me here. This is all still new to me."

"Yes, it takes all of those things and sometimes more. Sometimes sacrifices, like Spiros committed. But those deaths had to occur by a human hand to pull the Rissu here. This one is different. Pulled by another method."

He rubbed his eyes. "What kind of...wait, wait, wait.

I'm going down the wrong path here, right? Let me back up." He sat back down and began typing on the keyboard. "If we have access to Metro, we have access to my files."

Shia nodded. "Yes, your access is still the same. It will appear as though you've logged in from your home system."

"Even without my hardware token?"

"Jace has cracked all the encryption algorithms. Your access will seem appropriate."

He nodded, an absent tribute to her technical talents. "You're good. Any chance Jace comes with a Buck Rogers coffee maker?" Ryan began typing quickly, pausing only when the computer screen couldn't keep up with him.

Laughter wrapped around him when a small section of the desk opened up with a steaming mug of Columbia's finest. Shia merely smiled when one opened on the side of her desk with her favorite tea. She went back to visibly searching the markings on Tyler Daniels body in the photos Jace pulled up on screen.

Ryan raised his index finger, drawing a line in the air. "Point for you." He typed for a few more moments, then stopped and stood as Tyler Daniels' case file filled the screen. "Okay, demons don't accidentally come to reality. They are called, or summoned, like you said. That's supposed to require some elaborate ceremony or a sacrifice or what criminal psychologists call 'a compelling event.' If I'm going to figure this out, I need to know one thing first. Why this kid?"

"Grudge. Crime of passion. He offended someone, probably female, in the worst possible manner." Shia hated to say it, but most crimes were crimes of passion or of greed. "This kid had nothing. He had to have taken something from someone."

Tattoo on right upper arm. Birthmark, lower left leg.

Dog bite scar on the web between his thumb and index finger on his left hand. She continued to make notes on screen for the files as she chronicled them. Serrated knife scar down his right forearm. This kid had grown up hard, on the streets.

Ryan scowled. "That would constitute a compelling event." He flipped the case notes. "Daniels hasn't hit 18 yet, thankfully, or his record would be wiped clean. He's been bounced around in the foster system, and he's got a rap sheet, but it's mostly vandalism, petty theft, and arson. If he did assault a female, or females, he got away with it, according to the justice system."

She nodded her chin at the screen where she was compiling notes. "He's been pretty rough and tumble. If he'd hurt another kid in the foster system, it likely wouldn't have been reported. Those kids don't talk. And when they do, they're ignored."

"Are we both thinking victimized female, Detective?" She hit a few more keys and narrowed Jace's search parameters even more on the demonology database.

"Somebody has to hold a grudge, one big enough to call a demon to come alive right-the-hell inside of this kid. I get Daniels wasn't a good kid, but, damn. How deep do you have to hurt a person to bring about this kind of punishment?"

Shia ran though old literature passages in her head. "The daemonic is any natural function which has the power to take over the whole person. Sex and Eros, anger and rage, and the craving for power. Rollo May stated that in his text on Love and Will."

Ryan lifted his eyes to meet hers.

"Some of these kids have a lot of rage." She added.

Ryan nodded absently. "He got away with it. No wonder she's so hurt. She was either too scared to report it, or she did, and we let her down." He sank back in his chair. "Holy shit, Shia, we gotta find this girl."

"Agreed. Suspect is a girl. However, I'm going to have to make this one go away." She cut Ryan a glance. "Right now, we have no way to prove she's connected. No physical evidence or should I wait?"

He stood and was already heading to the door. "There wasn't a sign at the scene. Video, footsteps, interviews, all turned up empty. Say the kid mixed up something from The Anarchist's Cookbook or something. Hell, you'll know how to cover it better than I would. I'll start interviewing Tyler's stops in the foster system. Somebody has to know something, and if they do, I'll find it."

Shia nodded, not even bothering to respond, already putting the steps in motion with Jace's help. By morning, well, later morning, the case would be closed, on a scientific basis. She frowned, not liking the outcome, but knowing in the end, she needed to do it to find the demon. Somewhere, she'd find a way to make it up to Tyler Daniels' soul, even a bad kid needed redemption.

"Stay in contact, Detective." She called out. The door slammed hard, Calder's frustration getting the better of him.

"Ryan" She whispered.

The photos of Tyler Daniels' unique skin markings remained on screen as she stood up and stretched. Jace would run the reports. She needed sleep. With a demon to hunt, she needed to reserve her strength.

CHAPTER 7

For the hundredth time, Shia wondered how she'd been talked to or even guilted into this. She knew she couldn't leave loose ends. The female in her outweighed the warrior in her in this instance. She took a deep breath before lifting her hand to knock on the door of apartment 3A. Three flights of stairs, the elevator and front entry way heavily guarded. Nothing for her to get past security. She couldn't chance being seen, or stopped and questioned. She wasn't supposed to know about the location, and she didn't need what she was about to do to lead back to her, better to rely on her shinobi skills and conceal herself in plain sight.

She knocked.

There was a long pause. The sound of feet shuffling on hard wood floors grew closer. She waited, as the footsteps neared, then stopped. The door provided no peephole, but certainly cameras must have the entryway covered.

"Who's there?" came a nervous reply.

"This is Dr. Ronin." She took another deep breath. "Ryan sent me to help you."

That last part burned in the back of her throat. Victim,

past lover. She knew she had no claim to the detective, but she was female enough and warrior enough to know she didn't like the thought of him near another woman. Especially another female warrior, albeit one of this time, one so much better suited to his normal lifestyle although mentally bent over recent demonic events.

"Ry...Ryan?" Came the response, hardly audible through the door.

Shia bit back a sigh; at once sorry for the trauma the agent had been through and impatient enough to want to get the helping part of her over. "Yes, Agent. If you let me in, I can help."

She adjusted the light backpack on her shoulder and toyed with the thought of picking the locks. She could move fast enough the traumatized agent might not shoot her before she could snare her.

Another long pause, followed by the sounds of several deadbolt locks being turned. The door opened slowly. "Please, Dr. Ronin, please come in." Despite centuries of experience with victims, this moment was never easy. Shia looked at the woman in the doorway. FBI Agent Felicia Simone looked years older, paler, and frail. She stared at the floor instead of meeting Shia's eyes. She looked, in a word, hollow.

Shia moved slowly, careful to keep any movements soft, slow and calculated. The woman before her was lost, lost in a dimensional rift with which she had zero preparation to deal.

"Thank you, Agent Simone." She bowed slightly. "I am honored you allowed me to come help you."

Felicia looked up for a moment and then back at Shia's shoes. "Did you come to arrest me?"

"Arrest you?" Shia stopped in momentary surprise. She actually hesitated. "Agent, I'm here to help you. Why don't we sit down and you tell me why you think

I'd be here to arrest you?"

Felicia turned and walked slowly toward the main room of the apartment. Shia shut the door behind her and locked it, memorizing the motion. If she needed a quick exit, she wouldn't be sidetracked by a myriad of locks. She followed Felicia into the main room, struck by its condition. It was completely empty, save one square pillow in the center of the room. When Felicia spoke, her voice echoed, even in such a small space. "I...I killed him."

"You killed who, Agent?" Shia's voice dropped into a soft, hypnotic realm. Energy began to dance and hum around her. "Why don't we sit?"

Felicia shook her head, still facing away from Shia. "I confess. If that's what you want, I confess. I stabbed Alexander Spiros in the back. Over and over again." Her voice grew louder, along with the tinge of pain in every word. "I killed him. I killed him." Suddenly, she turned, eyes red with tears, teeth clenched. "But, you have no idea what he did to me. The things he did to me. He cut me. He hurt me. He humiliated me. He...he...he...." She dropped to her knees and sank her head into her hands, sobbing.

Shia looked over the agent's head with sympathy. She'd been there once, so very long ago, another lifetime, another several lifetimes ago. "Felicia, some men deserve to die, whether at our hands or another. You were not only protecting yourself, but defending others from having it happen to them, by the same man. You are not at fault."

The woman had sidetracked him enough Shia had time to kill the Mother Rissu. That alone deserved a reprieve, an offering. Of course, she'd also killed the psychotic billionaire with Shia's dagger, which at that point, might have been the only reason the cretin died.

Felicia looked up, an ember of hope behind her eyes. "It hurts. It hurts so much. I want it to go away."

Shia set the bag she had with her down on the floor. She flowed down to the floor into lotus position, capturing and holding Felicia's gaze with her own. Energy sparked out and wrapped around her, slowly expanding to capture Felicia in its web as well.

"Felicia, I want you to look at me. In the eyes. It can go away, but you must focus on my eyes."

Felicia nodded slightly, enough to confirm she understood, and that the energy had reached her.

"I want you to go back to that morning, before Spiros, somewhere you felt safe. We're going to start there." Shia kept her gaze focused on Felicia's eyes, every so often allowing a slow and steady blink. "Tell me where that space is. When that time was."

She needed to rebuild the memories, create a scenario, a reasoning as to why the Agent now lived where she was, on the run from Spiros because of the data she'd obtained about his actions.

Felicia's eyes were slightly unfocused. "I was asked to investigate a homicide. I didn't want to, but then I looked at the case notes. The DC lead detective was Ryan, my Ryan. How could I resist?"

Shia nodded. Yes, she'd agree on the hard to resist... the charm, the singing at odd moments, and the bringing her hot tea. The man had a unique charm. She mentally shook herself. No, focus. "Yes, so I've seen. I need you to focus on the last moment, before the day shifted. Were you with Ryan?"

The faintest smile crossed Felicia's lips. "We were together. It was a hotel room. The same room where we had stayed undercover on a mission." She ran her hands over her arms. "The shower was so warm. I can still feel the heat on my skin. I crawled into bed and asked Ryan to join me. He was staring out the window, so protective, always looking out." She sighed, her mind in the moment, providing the trigger Shia would need.

Every nerve in her body went on full haze red alert before she forced herself to breathe. Now was not the time to have a purely feminine reaction. She needed to cover their tracks and set the story right so the humans would believe the right trail. Her shoulders twitched, she resorted to her early samurai training and forcibly blocked out all personal responses.

"He was gone in the morning, leaving you a note to take to cover. That's the reason you're here, hiding and waiting, so Spiros can't find you and the evidence." She applied a specific cadence to her voice. "You're waiting for the right time to take the evidence forward, to get it out there."

"I'm waiting here for the right time to present the evidence. Spiros was a murderer."

Shia smiled a slow smile. "Yes, Agent. You have all the evidence right here in your hands." She inched the backpack forward. "Photos, emails, even the court orders to do the searches. All conducted by you personally, undercover, and under orders." Ilsa had made sure the electronic trail was rock solid, as she'd done for every case in their past. "You moved here as a safety precaution. You didn't really want to stay here, so no furniture, no personal items, in case you had to leave quickly." Shia glanced around and then thought about it. "But, now you know you can take the evidence forward, and you can keep this as your home, safe and protected." And so very much easier for Jace to keep tabs on her and the conditioning.

Felicia looked around, a new light in her eyes. "My home?" She turned back to Shia. "This is what I've been waiting for. How did you know?" She leapt to her feat, clutching the backpack to her chest. "I have to get ready. I don't have a thing to wear!"

Shia's eyes widened as she was effectively forgotten. She swept up to her feet. "Agent!"

"You never saw me. If you happen to pass me, you might recognize me, but only in the morgue or on scene." She couldn't chance the Agent remembering her in battle, or her damn dagger. "If we pass in any company, I am nothing more than a professional acquaintance."

Felicia blinked, her eyes once again vacant. She nodded absently. "Of course. Will you forgive me? I have business to attend to. Can you show yourself out, Miss...um...I'm so sorry, what was your name?"

Shia smiled. Good. Success. She flipped the hood of her jacket up and over her head, pulling her face into the shadows. "Of course, Miss, so sorry to intrude. Have a wonderful day."

She backed out slowly, even going so far as to undo the locks behind her back with memory. She believed the restructuring took, but she wasn't going to chance it until events unfolded. Felicia needed time for the conditioning to set it.

She made her way beyond cameras and security back down the to street and the Impala waiting for her on the corner. She stepped in and seated herself when the passenger door opened.

She clicked the seat belt in place and flipped back her hood. "It's done."

Ryan nodded. He reached his hand to her once, then pulled it back, covering the stick shift. The car was miles down the George Washington Parkway before he managed a "thank you."

"She will be heralded a hero, Detective. Her mind is intact. Please take me home. I need sleep." Shia closed her eyes and leaned back against the leather seat, emotions and energy drained as her body and mind shut down. She should have waited, but she couldn't. She was done and could do no more. She could only hope Jace was monitoring her vitals and had the bots ready and waiting to move and sequester her until she regained consciousness. She'd expended too much energy and needed to replenish. Even an immortal had her limits. She'd reached hers.

Detective Ryan Calder changed lanes and course, answering Shia's wishes. He didn't need the artificial intelligence to chart his path. He knew where they were heading, even before he knew. The taillights of the Impala filled the first lights of the dawn, and then faded. In a moment, they had disappeared. Hidden in plain sight, as they were designed.

Breaking News – Department of Justice to Formally Charge Ixion Industries CEO with Murder
FBI Special Agent Felicia Simone speaks to the Media
(Photo courtesy of Associated Press)

935 Pennsylvania Ave, NW
Washington, DC

A special agent for the Federal Bureau of Investigation today announced the Bureau intended to file formal murder charges against one of the Government Defense Industry's most influential people. Alexander Spiros, CEO of Ixion Industries (NYSE:IXIO), is the lead suspect in an investigation into two separate homicides. "Despite the lack of a confession," Special Agent Felicia Simone stated to a startled media on Friday, "we believe the bureau has gathered indisputable evidence to prove Alexander Spiros' guilt in multiple murders that occurred in Georgetown in the period between July and October. We have issued a warrant for Mr. Spiros' arrest. His passport and assets have been frozen, and a team of investigators have been sent to his primary residence, Ixion Industries corporate headquarters, and his multiple vacation residencies."

The murders in question are those of Charles and Abigail Huang, a couple who resided in Georgetown. Abigail Huang was found dead at the historic "Exorcist Stairs" located at 36th and M St Northwest. Charles Huang was killed at gunpoint in Little Falls Park two weeks later. No other suspects were named in the investigation in which DC Metro partnered with Agent Simone and the FBI.

Interview requests with Alexander Spiros' family were not answered; however, Ixion Industries Chairman of Public Relations, Larry McElrich released a statement following the FBI press conference. "Alexander Spiros has a long record of innovation and integrity in government relations. He is a storied philanthropist and family man. He is a proud husband and father, and above all, a true patriot. Ixion Industries will do all we can to cooperate with this investigation and to clear any misunderstandings. Our companies, and our chairman, have always operated with a policy of accountability, and we will hold strong to that policy during this investigation."

Agent Simone's language was much more direct. "The Bureau has no other persons-of-interest. Anyone who has information on Alexander Spiros' whereabouts should contact my team at the toll line listed on the bottom of your screen. This is a matter of life and death."

The tip line is 1-888-555-4808. Anonymous inquiries may contact this station at info@wxxx.usa.com.

Shattered plane found in Exuma Cays, Bahamas

One man aboard a small airplane that shattered in Exuma Cays waters has been identified.

By Chris Weitzel / THE WASHINGTON INSIDER

WASHINGTON DC – One man aboard a small single-engine airplane that crashed in the waters of the Exuma Cays in the Bahamas has been identified by airport officials.

The owner of the Beechcraft Musketeer was identified Monday morning as Alexander Spiros, the 53-year-old CEO of Ixion Industries. According to FAA records, Spiros is a licensed private pilot and has been for over 10 years.

Monday afternoon, airplane parts were being removed from the bay by rescue workers and will be examined by the investigators at the National Transportation Safety Board.

Chris Hadlock, the lead NTSB investigator in the incident, said officials were taking care to make sure no chemicals were leaking from the plane wreckage into the ecological preserve where the plane crashed.

The aircraft had taken off from Washington DC and was headed to the Exuma Cays, a private island owned by Spiros, but the pilot experienced engine difficulties a few miles out from the landing tarmac.

The 1968 airplane is believed to have landed nose first in Exuma Cays at 5:45 p.m. The plane shattered on impact. Debris was all that could be found of the wreckage.

Greg Garcia, spokesman for the FAA, said the plane was flying from Washington DC for an extended weekend on the island. According to his staff, Spiros wasn't scheduled to return to the Washington DC area until Thursday morning for an appearance with the Chief of Staff for the US Army. The details of his meeting are unknown at this point.

The FAA and the NTSB are investigating the crash. NTSB officials will be taking the wreck of the plane to inspect it for any mechanical malfunctions, Hadlock said. It is still unclear what caused the crash, he said. Investigators will also be reviewing radar data and the altitude changes in the plane to find out what might have caused the crash, he said.

Contact the writer: cweitzel@washingtoninsider.com or 202.555.5555.

CHAPTER 8

Driving was as involuntary to Ryan as breathing. He'd been around vehicles his whole life; tractors, ATV's, motorcycles, cars...big cars, little cars, muscle cars. There was a reason he loved his Impala. He worked on it himself. He knew every part, at least, until Jace made modifications. Another part of everything he had every known turned on its head. That was his life ever since she'd come into his life. He cast a quick glance to the passenger seat. Shia Ronin rested without a sound against the passenger window. Everything he had ever known changed in a blink.

The Impala pulled up to Shia's current residence. Jace confirmed Ryan's driving, but the detective hadn't needed the AI for a single turn. He'd been here once, and this was his city. He knew every turn, right down to the potholes. He shut off the engine and drew in a deep breath.

"Lady Shia is sleeping fitfully, Detective. I will provide access to the inner lair if you will carry her."

Ryan looked and caught himself staring. "Of course, Jace."

Her body weighed nothing in his arms, as if he had always been meant to hold her. She nuzzled subconsciously closer to him as he lifted her from the car. He smiled without meaning to. He took a few steps toward the warehouse and leaned his cheek against her dark hair.

"Shhhhh," he whispered.

Jace lit the path with motion lights. Ryan carried Shia's sleeping form inside, through the main hall and up the stairs to what the AI had described as the inner lair. He passed a gym with mirrored walls, hard wood floors, and weapons lining the wall. He carried Shia to her bedroom. In his earlier stint in the room, he hadn't noticed the furniture. Now, he allowed himself the time to glance around before settling her. The furniture was simple, a combination of bamboo and rice paper. He slowed his pace as he reached her bed. He lifted her in his left arm as he pushed the sheets back with his right. For such a powerhouse, she was a tiny thing. He laid her gently down, then covered her with the blankets and comforter.

Shia curled up beneath the covers. Ryan watched her and waited. In that moment, there was no supernatural and no reality. There was simply the innocent, trusting woman sleeping in front of him. He wanted nothing more than to stay and watch her...so peaceful, without movement or intent.

"Detective, there is one more task I must ask you to fulfill." Jace's voice seemed to pour into the room from every direction.

"Fine," Ryan whispered. "What?"

A panel shifted on the nightstand, revealing a syringe. The liquid inside seemed to change from colors to metallic shades. "Lady Ronin requires an injection to restore her proper energy levels."

Ryan shook his head. "She needs to sleep, Jace. Let her rest."

"Negative, sir. This chemical compound is precisely formulated to Lady Ronin's metabolism. It will reduce her recovery time and maximize her productivity."

Ryan shifted his gaze around the room. "She needs rest, not some chemical compound, Jace. Let her listen to her body."

"This isn't my direction, sir. This is what Lady Ronin commanded of me. She fulfilled your request earlier. I ask you fulfill hers now."

Ryan lifted the needle from the nightstand. "Those aren't your words."

Jace replied quietly, "No, sir, they are her orders."

He walked closer to Shia's sleeping form. "Fight a little, Jace. Next time, ask her to program you with a little gusto." Ryan lifted Shia's arm from beneath the covers. He paused only a moment before injecting her with the shot.

Shia shot up in bed. She grabbed Ryan's arm, and on instinct, he grabbed hers. She stared into his eyes. They were captured, focused only on one another. She blinked once, a recognition flowed across her face, then disappeared, and her grip lessened on him. He caught her as she drifted back down to the bed.

Ryan guided her down, measuring her breaths. He pulled the comforter up to cover her shoulder. With a sigh, he stole one more gaze at her before he stood and walked from her sacred, private, inner lair as he had before.

Jace's voice spoke to him, but it was an echo. "You are quite fortunate, sir, Lady Shia has a very deliberate killing strike."

The Detective stalked down the stairs and walked to the chair in the lab-office that Shia had designated for him during his last visit. "Isn't that reassuring? You ever heard of a Monday Morning Quarterback, genius?"

"I can research the topic, Detective."

"Save it, Jace. Now be a good boy and let me work."

Ariel caressed the book in her lap. The leather was soft under her fingertips.

She'd hidden it deep in her backpack, so even when her foster parents searched it...they'd found nothing. She'd been tense. The book was big, but they rarely actually looked at the books, only looking for hidden stash, Ziploc bags, weed, drugs, or cash she couldn't account for. She'd learned long ago what she could hide in plain sight and what she couldn't.

She could leave the book out, under something, and they'd never suspect a thing. She took the harassment, the 'where were you's' and murmured an apology. She even offered up a beautiful jade carving of a dove she'd found in a Chinatown vendor stall to her foster mother.

Her "mother" stopped harassing her, instead, oooohing and ahhing over the detail, the thoughtfulness and the reminder to get her homework done.

With the distraction, Ariel retreated to her room. Thankfully, in this house, this was her room and hers alone. No one entered unless she asked or granted permission. Her current foster parents were far more gracious than those she'd had before.

She didn't hate them. They were trying to be good people. She was far too damaged. She could love them or hate them. They weren't hers. They just were in a long line of people who'd tried to claim her, own her, kill her.

No more.

"Ariel." The voice whispered through her head. She looked around for her book, knowing well enough it was hidden in her backpack. The book comforted her, kept her sane, focused. She settled some knowing it was on her back. She had power.

"Go to your room. We need to talk." The voice whispered.

She tried to make small talk with her foster mother, finally claiming she had homework to do and retreated to her room. As the eldest foster kid, she had a room to herself. Sometimes, her age worked to her advantage.

She sat down in the windowsill and opened the book in her lap. Her backpack discarded by the locked bedroom door. She had at least two hours before they bothered her for dinner.

"You were right to call me here, Ariel. I can feel your pain. I can feel what has been done to you. Your soul vibrates in harmony with mine. We have much to accomplish together."

Ariel's head lifted, before her, in the center of her room, stood a vision in red, red gold hair, the body of a goddess. "Who are you?"

The voice itself seemed to smile. When Ariel heard it speak, the voice was her own. "He hurt us. He lied to us. We were humiliated. We were ridiculed." The red eyes stared right into Ariel's. "I am what you wanted. I am your freedom. Together, we will make it right. Together, we will grow strong. We will find vengeance. I will keep you safe." The eyes turned sympathetic. "We will find love. Nothing will ever hurt us again. We will have our family."

Ariel dissolved into the eyes. She'd been hurt. So many times. She was done. She'd been the brunt of too many jokes...she laid her hands down on the journal and gave in, wanting someone, something to step in and take care of her.

"Focus," the voice replied. It was her voice, but her voice on multiple octaves. It was wind chimes. It was the rage of an inferno, but it was still her voice. "Focus on the one who hurt you. Find his heart."

She spoke once more, and their voices were united.

"Focus on his soul."

CHAPTER 9

The regulars called her Sapphire Blade. She was the best dancer at the Gold Club. She commanded the top slots on the schedule. Friday and Saturday nights every weekend, and one service industry night, aptly named SIN, every week. Businessmen, congressmen, and the occasional cabinet member made it a point to see her perform and to pay for her appearance at their table between shifts.

Sapphire worked a brass pole the way a lion tamer worked his whip. Her lion was the passion of every man in the room, and she had no problems gathering its attention and devotion. Her legs were long and tan, and she was tall, even without the glass heels. Her arms were toned from years perfecting her craft. Her blonde hair fell to the middle of her back. Tonight, she wore her signature blue lipstick and eyeliner as she danced.

Sapphire's performance tonight was unlike anything she'd ever done. From the moment she grabbed the brass pole and cast a seductive smile over her shoulder at the men nearest the stage, something else took over. The bass pounded through her body. The guitars electrified every pore of her skin. She mouthed the words to the song on the club's sound system, even though she had never heard it before.

Sapphire Blade grabbed the pole and swung herself upward, the muscles in her shoulders popping. She spun several times, landing with the grace of a tigress inches away from a man seated at the closest table. She snatched his tie and pulled him close enough to share a breath before pushing him away, flashing a seductive smile from her bedroom eyes. The others at his table poured dollar bills onto the stage as if she'd held them at gunpoint. Fives, 10's, 20's, and the occasional $100 hit the stage at her feet. She swung upward again, hanging upside down, with only the leverage of an ankle to keep her from falling. She spread her arms outward, as if spreading outstretched wings. Her bare breasts heaved in the changing lights. The observant fan should have recognized the small tattoo at the base of her neck, but every man in the crowd focused on her curves, her natural feminine graces.

The song ended, and the club dropped to darkness. The bouncers immediately pulled out flashlights, and the shouts of the waitresses shot through the air as patrons took the opportunity to grope the staff. Seconds later, the lights and music regained form. A few overly affectionate patrons were tossed down the back steps, but, for the most part, the night progressed according to schedule.

Sapphire changed into a tight-fitting, translucent dress, and stepped to the end of the girls' collective changing room. The club coordinator met her at the door, wearing all black, right down to the monitor in his ear.

"Table 6," he said, handing her a slip of paper and a large tip.

Table 6 had won the bidding war, and with it, a visit from the prize dancer, at least until her next shift. Sapphire took the paper and smiled. Table 6, all as she planned.

She checked her make-up once more and exited the backstage area, striding confidently to Table 6. She extended her hand, palm down, to the handsome blonde in the gray suit sitting at the closest seat. "Good evening, gentlemen. Do you have room for one more?"

They responded to her every wink, nod, giggle and feigned shock as the alcohol made them braver. Sapphire removed a grip or two, but made certain to be playful each time. Every once in a while, she returned her long lashes to the blonde who introduced himself as Mason Cofield. That was a few drinks ago. By the time Sapphire finished two more shifts, most of Mason's friends had cleared out, and he probably couldn't spell his own name.

She sat next to him after her final shift. The only others left at his table were a drunken co-worker and the dancer silently stealing his credit cards, phone login, and credentials. Sapphire had no desire to be that blatant, not with all the cameras recording the club's every movement. She pulled Mason into a surprised kiss. In an instant, he was as drunk on her energy as he had been on two hours of shots and beers. Her eyes met his, and he nodded without a word.

Sapphire guided Mason to his BMW 7-series. She eyed the expensive automobile, not bad for a twenty-something, pampered, corporate clown from a rich family. He had told his friends over a dozen times about the bright future he had with the company. A smile crossed her blue-painted lips. Poor Mason. He couldn't be more wrong. The two slipped into the backseat, Sapphire gliding over the polished leather. Mason fumbled his way to her, never in control, never wavering in his focus, such was her energy.

She wrapped her leg around his waist, pulling him close. Her hands caressed his chest. She reached a hand into his hair to pull him close. The desire was tangible, undeniable. It was the moment when lust became carnal, relentless. It was a need now, no longer a want. This was her moment. Her eyes flashed in the darkness, and she whispered, "Kiss me."

Mason Cofield dropped to his knees in the gravel, trying to stop the bleeding from his neck and from his abdomen. His eyes rolled back in his head, and the seizures gripped him before he fell. Sapphire watched him suffer, licking his blood from her nails. He wasn't the one. He didn't, couldn't, offer the true love Ariel sought so desperately. He was a good appetizer, though. Transparent. Desperate. Hungry.

The Succubus changed her form. Leaving her host was a disappointment, but tonight wasn't about fulfilling Ariel's wish. It was about satisfying an appetite that had gone centuries without a bounty. She stopped for a moment and let Sapphire's corpse drop to the gravel in the process. Licking her lips, she changed her energy pattern and returned to the desperate young woman who had granted her entry into this world.

Washington, DC had a long and varied list of history and culture. Of all the districts, Georgetown offered the widest variety. It was home to cathedrals, universities, rock bars, gay clubs, Blues houses, multimillion-dollar riverfront establishments, an underground mall, five star hotels, and quirky shops that catered to runners, bikers, and the broad range of nationalities who came by. Every style of food was represented in the restaurants, and it was all "authentic" with names right from the cultures. Georgetown was a study in variety, and it certainly played host to its variety of gentlemen's clubs. More than a dozen establishments existed at any time somewhere along M Street or Wisconsin Avenue.

The dirtier clubs were hardly about the dancers at all. They were usually fronts for the drug trade. There were the traditional places offering specials for bachelor parties and 21st birthdays. There were high-end places with back rooms where beautiful women fulfilled very specific, and very expensive, requests. The Gold Club was one of these. There was a tiered system to the gentlemen's club ecosystem of the Nation's Capital. Sapphire Blade was one of the top shelf offerings of the Gold Club. Naturally, her identity leaked out before the police even arrived on scene.

Sapphire's murder would have made the headlines, except a bigger fish had stolen the show. Alexander Spiros, CEO of Ixion Industries and prime suspect in two murders had died in a small-engine plane crash just north of his private island.

Ryan scoffed. Shia made good on multiple promises. Agent Felicia Simone had all she needed, and all she needed to forget, to come out a hero in the case. Shia's lithe redheaded sister staged the scene so no body would be found. It was all wrapped up nice and tight, right down to the bow. Ryan laughed at himself. The sisters had a few hundred years head start on him. He had a lot to learn if he was going to remain in their realm.

Ryan chirped the Impala's siren to life to part the gathering crowd blocking the entrance to the Gold Club's rear parking lot. A few people moved, but others ignored the siren, as they ignored all police-related matters. He slammed the horn, drowning out Elton John's "Goodbye Yellow Brick Road" on the radio. The others cleared the way with obviously ruffled feathers. The detective pulled his car between a marked cruiser and the ambulance. He opened the door and hunched his shoulders at the chill in the air. The sun was out, somewhere behind thick, gray clouds, and it did nothing to take the edge off of the bitter cold. He pulled his coat tight around his neck, armed the car alarm, and walked toward the crime scene.

Ryan ducked under the police tape, getting a decent view despite the swarm of first responders, medical examiners and uniforms. A sleek, silver BMW with the back door open. Blood everywhere. A blonde guy in a suit laid face down on the gravel. The song lyrics echoed in his head. "Maybe you'll get a replacement. There's plenty like me to be found."

A few steps away, a tan woman with blonde hair and blue makeup lay on her back, lifeless eyes staring up at the winter sky. Ryan cursed. The world didn't have many replacements for Washington's top exotic dancer. The reports were true. Sapphire Blade was dead.

"Jesus, Mary and Joseph," a deep voice muttered as he approached. Officer Patrick O'Shaughnessy shook his head and looked at the detective.

Ryan stifled a smile at the veteran's attitude. "Double homicide. This is going from bad to worse, Sarge. Anything to add?"

"Not much," the older patrolman replied, "looks like some extracurricular activities got intruded upon. Young, rich, white guy got slashed to ribbons. No idea what took out the stripper. We figure she maybe has a family history of something of a bad ticker. Not a scratch on her."

Ryan nodded. Of course, stone cold dead, but not a scratch on her. He opened the photo app on his phone and took a few pictures, knowing Jace would add them to the growing pool of evidence. Tyler Daniels didn't have any entry wounds. The only exit wound was him having been ripped apart. Now, he was staring at a professional gymnast-turned-stripper whose body had suddenly given up the ghost. "Anything else, O'Sho?"

"Off the record?"

Ryan looked up at the Irishman. "Off the record."

Sergeant O' Shaughnessy looked at him. "When did women start doing the..." He whistled and swished his fingers side to side above his crotch.

Ryan raised an eyebrow. "You mean shaving?"

O'Shaughnessy shook his head. "It's not natural. Why would a women intentionally strip away what God..."

"Pat!"

"Yeah, Detective?"

Ryan drew his hand across his throat in a mime motion to kill the conversation. "We never had this conversation."

"But..."

"Go give your statement, Sarge, and keep it clean."

Sergeant Patrick O'Shaughnessy looked hurt as he turned to face the growing swarm waiting outside the police tape. Ryan turned, waving his hands in the air in front of his face. He prayed for some mental Lysol wipes to remove the exchange from his brain. He was going to have nightmares about this, and his friend, O'Sho, was to blame.

"Fuck it," he cursed under his breath. He shook his head once more and headed to the pair of dead bodies adding to the new case.

Detective Ryan Calder belted orders at the young medical examiner hovered over the body of one of DC's relished dancers. The ME backed away, raising his hands in front of him to avoid conflict. Ryan snapped at the amateur.

"Detective, please. Don't growl at my staff. Jordan, back to the lab so I can transfer data as I find it. Good job and I'm sorry you were called out on my shift. I was still recovering from the previous night." Shia's voice whipped out and wrapped around both men.

Ryan fought surprise when he turned to face her. He clenched his teeth to avoid the first response that reached his brain. He shifted away from the junior examiner and walked to pace her, his boots crunching in the snow. "You're supposed to be asleep."

"I was. Jace woke me. This is a complete map to our current case. I can't sleep it away." Shia stepped in, camera at the ready, snapping pictures, equally sure Jace recorded every instance and nuance from the small camera on her lapel. She side stepped around the bodies, taking in every angle.

Shia nodded. "Crime of passion. Man ripped to shreds. Woman, no signs of trauma on her." She snapped a few more pictures and then stopped, hunched over in the snow, and hovered.

Ryan watched her move. "No signs of trauma. Why is she dead, then?"

"Flip her over." She whispered with her camera at the ready.

Ryan donned his gloves. He knelt down next to the body. The snow crept through his clothes and bit at his skin. He inhaled, then pushed the dead figure of Sapphire Blade onto her stomach.

Shia moved forward, he gloved hand lifting the woman's shirt, moving aside her shirt and lifting her hair, there. She snapped a picture. A mark. A symbol.

"Got it, Detective. Flip her back." She said. "I have an idea. It isn't pretty, or likely to be pretty for a while. I need DNA swabs of everything."

Ryan scowled. "Our killer didn't leave footprints. It didn't leave DNA. You've got something else, right?"

He complied, moving Sapphire's body back into the chalk outline, his eyes never leaving Shia's.

"There's DNA, look for the stretch goal. You'll find it, or I will. Part of my job." She nodded at him. "I've got something else. I think. Don't think because we don't have prints, we don't have DNA. Please, don't think that." She took out a test kit and swabbed the inside of Sapphire's mouth. She carefully placed the kit back in her bag.

He cut her off. "No, I trust you. We have to stop this. Now."

She nodded. "Let me get the data here. I'll feed some of it to Jordan at the precinct, let him do his job and take the rest back to the warehouse. Meet there when you're done? I'm sure Jace has already given you access codes." She lifted an eyebrow, but a hint of a smile crossed her face.

She shifted and took a few more pictures, and despite his instincts, he let her work. Detective Ryan Calder stood amidst the snowfall, watching the crews work. Shia finished her work, as promised, and disappeared in the middle of the falling snow. When he turned back to the crime scene, everything was distant. "Jace has already given you access codes," whispered through his head. He struggled to wake up as he walked toward the Impala.

"Jace, pull up coordinates and access codes. We have a meeting to attend."

CHAPTER 10

"Jace, start streaming data back to the Metro PD office lab, encrypted of course." Shia strode into the computer room, dropping her bags to the side of the desk. Screens lit up on the desktop monitors and appeared on several walls. She pulled the swab from its container in her bag and placed it on the small platform raised on her desk. She didn't even flinch as it lowered and disappeared from sight. So much faster for her to do the analysis here rather than the office lab. DNA analysis flowed on one screen. A montage of photos started on another. The wall lit up with a map, pinpointing the two crime scenes. A list flowed up next to it including dates, points, times it would take to get to major transportation hubs. Shia watched the simulations as Jace ran them.

The program expanded to include any type of biochemical agent that may have been deployed. Jace had the capacity to map any type of attack on the city, including terrorist activities, dirty bombs, and chemical warfare. If desired, the program output would include considerations for transportation routes, public and private means of escaping the city, and the security details of the well-known celebrities and politicians. The haystack of data could be shuffled and sliced any which way. Right now, it was the needle Shia needed to find in the middle of that haystack of data.

Across the desktop, a demonology hunt still scroll and blinked.

Shia looked down. Finally, three hits.

"Cross reference these with the photos I recently uploaded, against the ones you were taking at the time too."

"As you wish, Lady. Detective Calder is approaching the perimeter." Jace replied.

Shia glanced at the map that appeared on the far wall. Her security perimeter. Sure enough a blue dot slowly approached the warehouse. She swore under her breath. His unmarked car was going to start to draw attention, especially with those who lived along the walls of her building. "Start erasing data. I don't want his car showing up on any surveillance. And open the garage doors, he needs to be parking inside, not out."

"Beginning data wipe sequences now. Garage access change completed," Jace replied.

Shia nodded as if the AI could see her, realized he could, and went back to the demon list. The list was her best shot at figuring out how to track the killing spree and her best bet on predicting the next step.

She probably should have been more worried she'd given full access to her domain to a human. She couldn't be worried about him. She'd learned long ago the Universe had its own plan, and she was a part of it. She would have to learn to take what came and deal with the consequences later. Ryan had started to see things on his own. It wasn't as if she'd set out to show him any of it.

She scolded herself for giving it a moment's thought. She'd never encountered someone so outside her realm being about to see it. Something flickcrcd out of the corner of her eye. Data streaming past, but it snared her attention.

"...and I couldn't pull them up on my phone or have you floating images up when I'm trying to drive. I told you, Jace, I'll ask you for certain info. You're like a pop-up ad dispenser from the future, for crying out loud." Ryan entered, arguing, apparently with the AI.

Shia tilted her head, her heart hiccupping for a moment before resuming a normal pattern. Damn it. He was a distraction. A helpful, knowledgeable, complete warrior distraction. Part of her demanded she focus only on the data in front of her and the feminine part of her demanded she stop and take a moment to enjoy the fact he'd walked into her domain, and it was just the two of them.

"You stated you wanted to be notified when the additional crime scene data was available, Detective." Jace stated.

"Not if it means I run a red light and kill some party goers in Adams Morgan, genius."

"Gentlemen, can we focus please?"

She said it more for herself than them as she bit back a smile at their bantering. Oh, it was heaven having Jace banter with someone other than herself. She felt... she couldn't even define it. She turned back to the data streaming across as many screens as she could physically get to show up in the room.

Ryan ran a hand through his hair. "Sorry, Einstein here almost made me wreck my car. I have no desire to find out what the airbags of the future feel like, thank you very much."

"Yes, he does that." She cut him a glance before returning to her demonology list. She stood taller as the photo stream popped up three images.

Ryan walked around behind her to view the screen,

the snow on his jacket melting away in the warm sanctuary of her private den. "What have we here?"

Three images, similar yet different appeared on the screen. A small, heart shaped mark at the base of the back of the neck on each photo.

"That's right above the C7, the intersection of the cervical and thoracic vertebrae on the spine." Shia frowned. "That's on all three vics."

"That's familiar," he said. "You pointed the heart out to me on Sapphire. I'd call that more than a coincidence. I mean, honestly, how many guys would have something so fruity in such a conspicuous location?"

"Most men wouldn't. This is our link. A female demon focused on love or revenge for love thus, the heart shape." Shia flicked her fingers over the screen, enlarging the images. "But, this female demon has to have a human portal."

"Think the human's a killer?"

"She may not have before, but she will now, or soon, if she's the one who called her." Shia fingers flew over the keyboard. "There are three demons with a tenant for passion, sex and pain." Images flowed up across the wall, covering the security map that had been there before.

"Our most likely demon suspect, based on this is a succubus. I can't tell you what branch yet."

She pulled up the images of the three most likely branches of demons.

She pointed to the first one. "Yuki-Ona. Japanese succubus. She is winter. White hair, dark eyes, usually wearing white. She is a lover of children and will respond to a call for a child with the correct incantation. She has the softest side of them all."

Ryan whistled. "She's the easy one? They get harder?"

Shia cut him a glance. "She, she might let a victim go."

"The others won't." Another image appeared on screen. "A traditional succubus has sex with sleeping men, a little more of a reach. Our vics haven't been all men and sleeping, but still, depending on the individual succubus. Their tendencies, like most women, are their own."

"'...and lead us not into Temptation...' Hardcore stuff, literally."

She nodded. "And the last, the one I really hope we're not facing would be a Lilin. The daughter of Lilth and Adam, the focus of a succubus, steals children, but only haunts the night. She can take any shape, form. She is in essence, ethereal. Called for a specific task, but not bound by that task."

"Daughter of Adam? You mean, THE Adam? Book of Genesis Adam?" Ryan moved his eyes from the screen to Shia. "That's some serious hate. You ever face one of these before?"

"A Lilin? No. Succubus? Yes." She said.

"So, we..." Ryan paused as his phone rang. He looked down, and his entire body dropped with one look at the screen. "Damn."

Shia tensed at his response. "What is it, another victim?"

"Worse," Ryan answered as he lifted the phone to his ear, "a priest."

Shia bit her lip as Ryan turned away from her.

"Calder." She watched him throw his arms in the air. Few people could act as Ryan's puppeteer, but she knew one who had the art down to its simplest form. "Padre, what a pleasant...what? No. That's tonight?"

Ryan found a nearby wall to rest his forehead against. "Yes, yes, of course I asked her. The problem, Padre, is that we're in the middle of a multiple homicide invest... yes...the children. Okay, okay, okay." He stood back up to his full height, his eyes meeting Shia's. He began nodding slowly as his tone changed. "Of course, Padre. We will be there, as you asked." He nodded slower, trying to get Shia to do the same. "Of course. For the children."

Shia's eyes widened as Ryan drew closer to her. She tilted her head in question.

Did the Detective just promise them both to something rather than their investigation?

Ryan ended the call, groaned, and proceeded to bite his phone.

"Oh my god, did you just...? What is it?" Shia knew her eyes were wide.

Ryan closed his eyes, letting the phone drop from his clenched teeth into his open palm. "Remind me he's a Holy man, and I really do love him, and his really is all about the children."

She softened. She liked Father Munoz. "He's asking you something. You can't ignore him. He's a man of faith. And he has power, his belief helps to keep those children safe, protected, and on the right path."

The detective dropped into the closest chair, running a hand through his wet hair. He stayed silent, staring at the floor.

She took a deep breath. "Ryan. He is not in danger. The children are safe. His request cannot be life impacting. The man stood up to a Rissu. He is owed our protection. Our gratitude. What is he asking for?"

Ryan kept his head down. "He called me a few days ago, asking me to attend the church's Winter Festival. I guess they don't want to call it Christmas or anything too locked in to a specific denomination's holiday. I don't know. He said it would mean a lot to him if I showed up." Ryan looked up to meet her eyes. "He asked for me.

The children asked for you."

Shia's entire body stilled. "They what?"

"The children said they like it when you were around. When Father Munoz asked if he should invite me, they said he should invite you, too." He stood and took a few steps closer. "So, what do you say, Lady Ronin? Do we have a date?"

Shia looked at the data streaming around her. Every known scenario she or Jace could think of flashed across the screens. She stopped and took a deep breath. The young ones had asked for her. It had been so long. She'd taught the little ones, so very long ago. She missed them.

"Ok, Detective, give me the afternoon."

The invitation said the open reception at the Winter Festival began at 6pm. The children's performance was scheduled for 7:30, giving guests plenty of time to mingle and meet one another. Naturally, it began snowing at 4pm. Ryan hung the Cloutier suit jacket in the back of the Impala. He wore the rest of the suit, along with the new Salvatore Ferragamo shoes, as he guided the unmarked car through Northwest DC to Shia's private lab.

"Would you like me to inform Lady Ronin you are near?" The AI asked politely, without filling his windshield with any graphics.

Ryan smiled. "I have a feeling she knows, but let's be gentlemen, Jace. Ring her and let her know. I'll be there in a few."

Ryan guided the Impala into the open garage moments later. He left the car and stepped quickly to the lab door. He reached for it, and Shia opened it seconds before his hand found it. The door opened, and Ryan stopped.

Shia stood before him, hesitant, in a blue gown. The blue silk caressed her curves. No way she was hiding her swords in her dress. Or anything else for that matter.

"Ryan." She said.

He gulped, forcing his eyes from her body to her face. "You look amazing."

"I am really hoping I'm not overdressed. Jace assures me I'm not." She looked unsure, hesitant.

He tried to stop the smile that crossed his face, but couldn't. "I guess I have to agree with Jace for the first time. I think you're perfect tonight."

A smile started across her face, "And entirely in your hands tonight, Detective. This dress, well, it doesn't allow me to keep myself very well defended."

He nodded, empowered by her very presence. He extended an arm, crooked at the elbow. "If you're ready, Lady Ronin, I would welcome the opportunity to escort you to a one-of-a-kind event."

She took his arm, her smile matching his own. They walked silently to the car. He opened the passenger door, and she sat down, her long legs filling the space between the leather seat and the floorboard. Ryan closed the passenger door, walked to the driver side and sat down in the driver seat.

Moments later, they were on the road. Ryan cornered and shifted lanes in traffic as easily as he did on the open road. He knew every inch of the Impala. He even changed slightly as the songs alternated from The Rolling Stones to Jethro Tull to Thin Lizzy.

"Your car is very top of the line, Detective." Shia said.

Ryan smiled, keeping his eyes on the road. He didn't dare steal a gaze at her. She was very, very distracting. "Actually, it's not even the latest Metro has to offer. I just take care of her, and I do some work on the side. I've been around cars since I was a kid."

He kept his eyes forward, but didn't hesitate to laugh.

"C'mon out, Jace, she knows already."

Shia slid a hand across the dashboard. "If I'd known what kind of things you'd take off on your own to do, Jace, I would have built better safeguards. Consider that fixed. Detective Calder is to have control over every aspect of his car, without your interference unless asked or life or death. Understood?"

"I will fulfill the detective's requests, in the order that I can best fulfill, my lady."

"Good." She settled back her seat.

Ryan looked at Shia and shook his head. "Known all along?"

She cast him a glance, "Suspected. Only way you could have found me. I am too well hidden. I've been doing this far too long."

"Point for you. Promise me one thing?"

She tilted her head, "What's that?"

Ryan stopped the car. The church filled the view outside his window. "Don't be so hard to track tonight. Just keep it simple, and stay near me?"

Shia smiled, an eyebrow raised, "Detective, you are my only source of defense tonight, I'm not going very far in this silk and no weapons. Although you might need to rescue me from an over exuberant child?"

A few dozen voices mixed among the acoustics of the church's greeting hall. Members of the congregation burst forth into hugs. New couples struggled to make introductions while coaching their children not to run in every direction. Ryan Calder and Shia Ronin entered the battlefield, anomalies among the population. They had no children, no wedding vows, no shared promise via baptism.

Shia's arm was crooked in Ryan's, even as they

registered at the table with the volunteer bottle blonde struggling to look fifteen years younger. They were eventually forced apart by members of the welcoming committee.

Ryan extracted his way out of two conversations to find her. Shia was nodding at an older woman, looking for an escape. As Ryan reached for her right elbow, another person grabbed her left.

"Dr. Ronin, you made it!" The voice came from a 10-year-old African-American child in the uniform of a ship captain.

Shia glanced down with a smile on her face, "Yes, Detective Calder made sure I did." She knew without a doubt, nothing could touch her within the sacred walls of the church.

And other than getting to spend time with Detective Calder, it was one of the only reasons she agreed to travel without her weapons, plus, the children had asked. She had a soft spot for them. She cut at glance towards Ryan, so very dashing in his suit and wished they had the church, the sanctuary to themselves instead.

"You're gonna love my part," the young man spoke as he looked up to her, "I'm Pirate Pete. Arrrr!"

Ryan met her gaze and let go of his grip on her arm with a wink.

Shia leaned down to face Pirate Pete, the young man she knew as Antwoine Bush, and smiled. "Promise you won't make me walk the plank?" She raised her open hands before her, and Pirate Pete smiled wide.

"If you're lucky, you may leave tonight...with your life!" He ran from the couple to the far end of the church.

Ryan reached a hand to Shia, who gripped his arm by the shoulder as she reached her feet.

"And this is less threatening than what I was doing?" She smiled up at him in delight rather than censure.

Father Munoz's voice ended their shared moment. "Lady Shia, Mijo, I am delighted you came together tonight to the children's performance."

Shia's eyes widened, and she quickly stepped to Ryan's side.

Ryan's arm reached out before he realized it, as he reached curled it around Shia's waistline. "Padre, please and thank you, we are grateful to be invited to the festival."

Shia nodded in agreement, standing strong next to Ryan's side, her head tilted as if she were listening.

Father Munoz smiled his knowing smile. "The show will begin soon."

The next several minutes passed as if in molasses. Ryan tried to mingle, but he could find no one else who fit his profile. He introduced Shia to new groups, where she continued to dazzle and delight. He would leave the interracial male-driven groups, only to pick up sarcasm and slurs. Apparently, most of the church's congregation wasn't familiar with the concept of a bilingual homicide detective.

Favorites among the whispers included "blanco diablo," "cochino," and "policia". Ryan shifted his gaze, weighing the players in the room. The audience was full of low-income, immigrant families. They hated the police. If he had been in uniform instead of a suit, they would have feared or hated him. Yet, all he wanted was to protect them and to keep them safe. Now more than ever, since he had been awakened to the enemies beyond reality.

He tensed, trying to subdue the anger. Shia smiled at him in the middle of her conversation, and he struggled to smile back. This was Holy ground. This was a place of peace. Still, he was the enemy, the bad guy with a target on his back. The dichotomy was painful.

"Shall we find our seats? I do believe the children are ready to start?" She asked.

A thousand protests died the moment he looked into her eyes. The peace he sought was suddenly inches away. A smile crossed his lips. "Best idea I've heard all night."

He followed, stealing glances at her lithe form accentuated by the blue dress. A few minutes later, they found their seats, and sat down. The crowd buzzed around them. The conversation was still mixed. Ryan caught a few snickers and side bars. He wasn't aware his right knee was bouncing up and down with negative energy until Shia put her hand on his knee.

Ryan looked up to meet her gaze.

"Please stop."

He blinked a few times, and his leg stopped bouncing. The house lights dimmed, and the choral instructor for the church stepped up to the microphone. "Good evening, ladies and gentlemen."

Shia leaned over and kissed Ryan's cheek as if it were the most natural gesture in their relationship. "Thank you," she whispered, leaning slightly into him as the festival began.

Ryan's heart stopped for a moment, and then he smiled, squeezed her hand a bit, and turned his attention to the stage.

CHAPTER 11

Tyler Daniels, the first victim identified with the string of homicides, was a troubled child. He loved rock music for its aggression and chaos. Maybe he had always loved chaos. Between the vandalism and arson charges peppering his juvenile record, there was a lot of chaos. Ryan finished his interview with Ryan's former foster mother. He left with a snarl on his face. He had grown tired of verbal insults and biblical references within a few moments. If he had lived in that house, he would have spray-painted and burned everything in sight himself.

Ryan slid into the driver's seat of the Impala.

"Would you like me to enter the next destination in the GPS system, detective?" Jace asked.

Ryan rubbed his eyes. "Give me a second, Jace. I need to clear my head, and I can't do that if I'm dodging anticipated Bibles."

"Yes, sir."

Ryan exhaled and left all other threats on his sanity at bay. He drew a deep breath into his chest, focused and exhaled. Each breath allowed him to focus more on Shia's face, the endless well behind her blue-black eyes. He could even feel the warmth of her smile. "Alright, Jace, who is our next contact?"

The AI replied, "Greenleaf Treatment Foster Care is next on the list of Tyler's caretakers. They are not open at this hour."

"Skip ahead. Who's next?"

"Douglas and Dorothy O'Brien were Tyler's next, and final, hosts among the social services network."

"Starting when?"

"March of this year. Their host rights completed upon Tyler's death. There was no formal adoption."

"Did they start the process?"

"Negative, detective. There was no progress to Tyler's adoption. His behavior, however, was much more controlled and consistent, following the medication regiment issued by the Greenleaf Treatment facility."

Ryan felt more focused, more determined, and yet more frustrated than ever. "Give me a readout on the medication regiment, and directions to the O'Brien residence. They won't like it, but I have a few outstanding questions I need to ask regarding Tyler's behavior."

The O'Brien residence was off of Decatur Place in Northwest DC. The area was best known for upscale cafe's like Zorba's, Bistro Du Coin, and the Cosmos Club. A few blocks away west led to a number of embassies. A few blocks south led to Dupont Circle, the capital's headquarters for the gay and lesbian scene. Places in this part of the city were pricy, even the condos. Ryan pulled the Impala next to the curb on the opposite side of the street and eyed the O'Briens' building. Not too shabby for a State Department Branch Chief and his University Professor wife.

"What do you think, Jace?"

"About the O'Briens, Detective?"

"Sort of. How does a kid apparently rising from the ashes of his past get involved in something that brings about a demon?"

"Difficult to say. There were no traces of spiritual energy at any of our previous stops. It remains very unlikely Tyler himself was the amateur summoner. As Lady Ronin stated, the summoner is more likely female, and one who suffered deep emotional damage."

Ryan slugged the rest of his Rev3 energy drink and tossed the can on the floor on the passenger side of the Impala. It clanged against two other empty cans. He smiled a moment, remembering the view of Shia's legs in that passenger seat earlier. "I'll keep that in mind while I interview the parents. Maybe they'll tip me off to someone."

He killed the engine, and with it, Pink Floyd's "One of my Turns." Roger Waters' voice hung in the darkness a moment before dissolving to silence.

"Here you go, Detective Calder." Douglas O'Brien called, entering the room with a tray in hand. A pot of hot tea and three cups rested atop it. Ryan stood to assist. Dorothy O'Brien remained seated, watching him through black-rimmed glasses. Douglas was a tall, slight man with dirty blonde hair graying at the temples. He smiled, grateful for the assistance. Ryan guessed him to be in his early 50's. He sported khakis, a dress shirt and sweater vest. Dorothy O'Brien wore a black blouse that matched her dyed hair. She had a gray knit skirt that covered her knees, even when sitting down. Maybe he'd caught them both before they had a chance to change after work. Ryan scoffed. He hoped they didn't dress like this all the time.

"Thank you, Mr. O'Brien. Your wife was telling me you're a fan of aviation?"

"Oh, yes," Douglas smiled widely as he poured the first cup of tea. "Did you see the framed pictures in the hall on your way in? I had the large one commissioned, a one-of-a-kind drawing of the Enola Gay. Beautiful work. The actual plane is out at the Udvar-Hazy Center in Virginia." He set the steaming cup of tea on the table in front of Dorothy.

"Douglas," she hissed, her eyes shooting daggers through him. He immediately picked up the tea and put a coaster under the cup.

Ryan watched as the couple had a silent exchange that looked a lot like a session in public humiliation. Skirt or no, he knew who wore the pants in this relationship. He broke the silence a moment later. This type of tension wasn't going to get any answers out of the O'Briens.

"I actually saw it for the first time last summer. I got suckered into being a chaperone on my nephew's field trip. That kid told me more about the Hiroshima bomb than I ever learned in school." He said.

Douglas nodded, smiling again. "Amazing what children learn and retain, isn't it?"

"You were asking about Tyler, Detective?" Dorothy's voice cut through the conversation, and Ryan pictured icicles in the room.

"Yes, ma'am," he replied, going back to the smart pen and tablet in his lap. "From everything I've read, Tyler's behavior was under control, and he was actually doing well in school under your care. Is there anything you can attribute to his success living with you?"

Dorothy O'Brien watched him for over a minute before replying. "Tyler had his challenges, but he was a good boy. I had to suggest a few modifications to his medication when he first arrived, but thanks to my guidance, eventually, he was able to overcome his flawed behavior. He was disciplined, attentive, and well-behaved under my care."

Ryan fake-scribbled some notes, writing only "wife

= megalomaniac" on the tablet. "Can you think of anything that would provide a distraction or obstacle in Tyler's behavior?"

Douglas started, "Well, there was one..."

"...Constant distraction," Dorothy finished, cutting her eyes at her husband again. "He was obsessed with music. He had delusions of being some rock star. We had a lengthy discussion about it. The result was his realization that rock stars are a thing of legend and history. He stopped that godawful racket and returned to his studies. Thank God. Last semester was the first time he'd earned higher than a D+ in American History."

Ryan nodded. He looked at Douglas, who cut him a sideways glance before staring at his tea in silence.

"Was Tyler close to anyone in particular while he was living here?"

Douglas looked at his wife instead of answering. She answered for them both. "Tyler's phone and computer usage were monitored very closely. He was allowed to communicate with classmates about schoolwork and with his representative in Social Services. Beyond that, we were certain to confront him on outside contact."

Ryan pretended to scribble some additional notes. The result was a female stick figure burning at the stake. "What about the other end of the spectrum? Did Tyler ever receive any threats while he was here? Did he have any enemies?"

"Tyler was a good child, recovering from a long period of self-inflicted torture. He was a good boy." Douglas stated without hesitation, tears in his eyes.

Ryan shifted his gaze to Dorothy, who didn't contradict her husband. "He was a good young man. We were blessed to have him in our family."

The interview ended a few questions and sips of tea later. Ryan apologized to the O'Briens for intruding on their time, expressed his sadness at their loss, and offered to lead himself out. Douglas followed under the premise of showing off the artist rendering of the Enola Gay in the hall. The two men stopped, facing the drawing. When Douglas spoke, it wasn't about aviation.

"She's distraught, Detective. My wife had an emotional tie to Tyler she's never had to anyone else, myself included. Through the grace of Social Services, my wife was able to be a mother. We, she, cannot physically conceive a child."

"That's probably because she has testicles," Ryan thought. "I'm sorry for your loss. I'll update you as soon as I know something."

Douglas nodded. "You asked if Tyler had any distractions."

"I did."

"I think there was a young girl with whom he communicated regularly. I heard him speaking on the phone sometimes, late at night. His voice had a tone that boys only take with girls." Douglas smiled, the dim light accenting the deep creases in his face. "Tyler was having these conversations from the first night he was with us. I think it might be someone he knew before he came here."

Ryan nodded. "I'll do my best to find out if that's true." He shook hands with the older man, finding his grip weak. "Thanks for your time, Mr. O'Brien."

While waiting for the elevator, Ryan snapped into his phone. "Jace, I need to start doing some digging on Tyler Daniels' phone logs. It looks like we might be able to build a timeline."

"Yes, Detective," the AI replied. "You may want to return to your car quickly. There is a person of interest spending a great deal of time on the driver's side of the vehicle."

Ryan left the O'Brien residence in a hurry, his breath steaming in the cold air. He made out the silhouette of a short, portly person next to his car. Jace had called the stranger a person-of-interest. Ryan was very interested in who was messing with his prized vehicle, and what how high his or her pain threshold might be. He strode to the middle of the road, leveling a glare at the figure huddled near his car.

"Get the hell away from my car right now." He commanded.

The figure turned and reached into his coat. He brought out his left hand. Ryan snapped his telescoping baton to its full extension and caught the stranger in the left wrist, sending whatever was in his hand skittering down the street. He raised his right hand to strike. A simple flick of the wrist and he could crush the man's collarbone, skull, or knee, if he was feeling creative.

"Ow! Wait, wait, wait." The man begged, holding his hands open in front of him. "Don't kill me."

Ryan snorted, lowering his baton slightly and gritting his teeth. "Carl MacAdams. Tell me what you were doing to my car."

The portly private investigator realized he was no longer a second from death and grabbed his throbbing wrist. "Relax, Detective. We're on the same side, remember?"

Ryan shook his head. Carl MacAdams was the lowest of lowlifes he had ever dealt with. "The same side? Last time we 'teamed' up, you tried to blackmail me."

"And I gave you your bad guy's head on a plate. You wouldn't have solved that case without me, and you know it."

"What were you doing to my car, jackass?" Ryan

stepped closer. The baton would be less of a resource at this distance, but an elbow or knee would suit just fine to put the egomaniacal investigator in a hospital room.

Carl looked to his left. "I was trying to figure out how to put that envelope in your car. I didn't want someone to steal it, so I didn't want to put it under your windshield wiper."

Ryan didn't turn away. "What's in the envelope?"

"Copies from my personal collection. I really want to help you nail the bastard who did this."

Ryan stepped back a bit. "The bastard who did what?"

"Christ, Detective," Carl replied, emphasizing every syllable with his arms in the air, "We're talkin' an American icon here. I mean this is a once in a lifetime case. We have to get to the bottom of this before the national media is all over it."

Ryan raised an eyebrow as Carl continued. The fat man began pacing as he dove into his monologue. "People are going to remember this. They're going to know where they were when they heard the news. I remember. I was in a biker bar, undercover, doing shots with a bottle blonde with great fake tits. But, that's not important. Well, it was then. Actually, maybe that's why I remember it."

"Carl."

"No, you're right. This is bigger than that, and those were pretty damn big."

"Carl."

"The news totally almost killed the mood. I couldn't believe it. This is the kind of thing that changes a generation. This is our Challenger disaster, our 9/11, our Waterfall..."

"Watergate."

"...Watergate. This is our Vietnam, our Kennedy assassination, all of it, all rolled in to one!"

"What the hell are you talking about, MacAdams?"

"This type of talent is once in a lifetime, man. Marilyn Monroe. Elvis. Jimi. Jim Morrison. John Belushi. Kurt Cobain. Jerry Garcia. Michael Jackson. Bettie Page."

"What?"

Carl MacAdams stopped pacing and stared at the detective. "Shit, man, don't you get it? Sapphire Blue is dead. She's gone, man."

Ryan lowered his baton, staring at the portly PI. "You came to me for this?"

"We can get the partnership back together, Ry. Think of it. Starsky and Hutch. Butch and Sundance. Castle and Beckett. You can be Beckett."

"Go home, MacAdams."

"You need me on this, Detective. I need to be a part of this."

Ryan slammed the baton to the ground, tip first, collapsing it back to its nine inch carrying state. "Go home, MacAdams."

"Ryan..."

The detective grabbed the fat man by the neck and arm, spun him around once, and then used his foot to sweep his feet out from under him. Carl fell on his butt in the street among the snow flurries. "This is my case. This is my investigation. Fuck with it, or my car, again, Carl, and what happens to you will be off the record."

"But..."

"Go. The. Fuck. Home." Ryan opened the door to the Impala and slammed it shut once he sat down. The car roared to life. Seconds later, it was gone, leaving Carl MacAdams sitting on his ass in the middle of Decatur Place.

CHAPTER 12

"This is Dr. Shia Ronin..."

Ryan cursed at the familiar introduction to Shia's voice mail. He swore he was going to swipe her damn phone and change the message if he didn't ask Jace to change it first. He changed lanes and continued down M Street. When the message beeped, he snapped, "Shia, I'm borrowing your AI. I think we have a lead. Let me know how things are going on your end."

He killed the connection.

"I have preliminary findings on Tyler Daniels' phone records, Detective."

"I'm listening, Jace."

"Yes, sir. Apparently to Blue Oyster Cult."

Ryan sighed heavily. "Mute the music and tell me what you've found."

"Given the timeline provided by Douglas O'Brien, the largest number of calls from Tyler to a single source is to Greenleaf Treatment Foster Care."

"Makes sense," Ryan answered. "Any idea who he's calling?"

"Negative, sir. The phone records end at a central switchboard. The calls are digital, and the facility uses

NAT and DHCP. The dynamic nature of the records makes it impossible to pinpoint the number he's called, because the number might change from week to week."

Ryan nodded, changing lanes again to avoid a courageous bike messenger, and a minivan showing children's programming to the back row of seats. "Let me rephrase that, Jace. Any idea who he is calling?"

"Detective?"

"Can you access the rolling roster of children in the Greenleaf facility?"

"Of course, sir."

"Good, then I need a list of girls who were there when Tyler was there, and are still there. He was calling that joint until he got mauled and killed, Jace. I need some visibility beyond the switchboard. I need to know who he was calling, not their address."

"I will begin calculations, Detective."

"Good," Ryan answered, "and while you're doing that, turn my damn music back on."

Greenleaf Treatment Foster Care began accepting visitors at 8am. Ryan was waiting, in his leather coat, arms crossed and breath steaming in the frosty air, when the orderly opened the front doors, promptly at 8:40. She offered no apology and rolled her eyes at the sight of Ryan's badge. Greenleaf was apparently visited by more cops than caring family members. And, the nurse on duty figured out how to build a callous on her soul and her attitude.

Jace had given Ryan eight names. Two were dead ends. Literal dead ends. Suicides...another statistic higher at Greenleaf than any other treatment center in the district. That left six girls. Ryan started down the roster. Four were still in the care of the Greenleaf staff. Two others had been placed with foster families.

The first girl was a deaf/mute who had never used a phone in her life. Ryan sat with her for about 20 minutes as she showed him the children's book she was writing. She communicated through a voice translator on her computer. By the end, Ryan was thankful for their time together, but certain she had no affiliation with Tyler Daniels.

Five girls left. One of them was close to Tyler. So close she wouldn't admit it. Ryan weighed the odds. He was a seasoned cop. He knew body language. Any of the five girls would deny knowing Tyler. He just had to read them to know which were lying to cover it up, and which weren't. Two interviews later, he eliminated two more suspects. The Bailess twins, Judy and Jody, had been desperate to meet Tyler when he was still at Greenleaf. They hadn't heard from him and were willing to give Ryan their number just in case Tyler wanted to call them.

That left three girls. Ryan checked the list. The names were Sylviana Gomez, Ariel Petrenko, and Eclipse, just Eclipse. Of the three, only Sylviana was still at Greenleaf.

Sylviana Gomez was an absolute firecracker. She was spray-painting her ceiling in a graffiti bomb when Ryan entered. "One Rhyme" from the R&B band, Arteless, filled the room, cranked on the radio like it was meant to fill an arena. Ryan cut the volume, and the only sound in the room was that of the Krylon spray can.

Sylviana looked down from her harness. "Yo, what gives?"

Ryan shook off the echoing bass in his head. "Metro PD. I need a few moments of your time."

Sylviana turned away and started painting again. "Fuck off, pig."

Ryan pulled the ESEE DPx HEST blade from his belt and tugged on the wire holding Sylviana in thc air.

"You got some answers, or you got some wings. Either way is fine with me."

The Latin girl huffed, then clicked the button that began her descent to the floor. She distributed a halo of profanities in Spanish on her way down. Ryan only grinned. Sylviana stood up once her feet touched down. She cocked her head at the detective. "Que Paso, Chancho?"

"Ever seen this kid?" Ryan replied, presenting a picture of Tyler when he first entered Greenleaf.

"No se. Is he some white kid pop singer?"

Ryan put the picture away. "Nah, just another white kid looking for a family. How long you been here?"

Sylviana slanted him a look. "Too long. Mi familia, they will come for me, when they need me."

"Ever run the halls with a kid named Tyler Daniels?"

The young woman shook her head. "Don't think I know him? Black kid? Sounds like a Black name to me."

Ryan nodded. "Go finish your work, girl. I like what you do with contrast. Just don't go tagging any trains in my town. I'd hate to bring you in for something so senseless."

She smiled. "You'd never catch me, Blanco."

Ryan only smiled as he closed the door to her room, the bass booming in his ears as he did.

He left his card for the nurse and the administration. The orderly at the desk put it on top of a pile of other cards, many of which looked like they'd been there for years. It was a crap job, Ryan understood, but dealing face-to-face with some of these folks was driving him past the point of reason. Ryan dropped into the driver's seat and started the Impala. "Jace, do you have locations on those other two girls?"

"Yes, detective, do you have a preference for the route chosen?"

"Get me to whoever is closest first."

"As you wish, Detective," The AI replied, feeding coordinates to the GPS system. Ryan rubbed his neck and put on his Ray Ban sunglasses. He reached down and brought the radio to life. Queen's "Somebody to Love" filled the interior. Ryan gunned the Chevy, pulled into traffic and off to the next stop.

A burly man with a thick, red beard and full head of hair answered on Ryan's second knock. "Can I help you?" he asked.

Ryan looked up at the man Jace had identified as Kevin Reilly. The man was enormous. Apparently his mother was Irish, and his father was a St. Bernard. "Metro PD, Mr. Reilly. I'd like to ask you just a few questions."

The big man snorted. "Make it quick. I'm on the job, and my daughter has disappeared again."

"Anything the police should be concerned with?"

"Yes," Kevin Reilly sneered. "It's Friday. She runs away almost every other Friday. Right after her Thursday night tantrum, and her overnight argument to drive my wife into tears." He ran a hand through his thick hair. "She'll be back. Someone will find her. They always find her, and she's back here like a bad penny to do it all over again."

Ryan nodded. "Would you care to fill out an official missing persons report?"

The big man leaned down to meet eyes with the detective. "No. If she doesn't come back, it will be the best thing for our whole family. Now, if you'll excuse me, I have a job to get back to."

Ryan thought it over. A few quick strikes would

take all the hot air out of the big Irishman, but they'd also likely cost him his hourly wage, at least until the swelling went down. Instead, he stepped aside. "Thanks for your time, Mr. Reilly."

The hotheaded man stormed past Ryan, pulling his toque on with a huff. A minute later, his big, black Ford F-250 left the driveway, leaving the road caked in mud from whatever construction site he was working on.

A 10-minute conversation with Mrs. Reilly was similar, with crying taking the place of rage. She wanted the best for Erica, the girl who had called herself Eclipse at Greenleaf. They hadn't managed to see eye to eye yet. She was convinced the girl was coming around. She allowed Ryan to look over the girl's room, and his quick investigation turned up no sign of the heart insignia or demon summoning paraphernalia. Erica mostly covered her walls with posters of HIM, Collide, and Nightwish.

A quick thank you and business card later, Ryan was back on the road. Jace updated the GPS and the detective headed to the last name on his list. Ariel Petrenko.

The two-floor residence was listed to Matthias and Leslie Shaw. Ryan walked to the door and knocked. He barely removed his fist from the white door when it opened. A man in khakis and a navy polo shirt met his gaze, a questioning look appearing on his face. "Can I help you?"

Ryan smiled. "Detective Calder, Metro PD. Is this a bad time?"

The man regained his composure, putting a hand on his chest. "You scared the devil out of me, Detective. We weren't expecting anyone at this hour. I'm so sorry. I'm Matthias Shaw." He extended a hand.

Ryan shook it. Shaw's grip was firm and polite. "I'm

looking into a missing persons case, Mr. Shaw. Is it alright if I come in?"

"Of course," Shaw replied. "Let me tell my wife you're coming in. I wouldn't want to startle her with Metro PD being here."

Ryan nodded and followed Shaw into the house. "Leslie! Leslie, dear, we have a visitor." Shaw called to the open stairwell. A few seconds later, a blonde woman wearing a sports bra and yoga pants appeared at the top of the stairs.

"Okay, be right down." She smiled. "Let me get decent."

The trio sat around the kitchen island. Matthias and Leslie held hands. Ryan held on to the steaming mug of coffee they had provided from their Keurig coffee maker. "So, how long has Ariel been under your care?"

"She came to us in February of this year," Matthias answered. "She is a quiet girl. We try to provide her with anything she needs."

"We care for her very much." Leslie added.

Ryan slid the picture of Tyler across the table. "Ever seen this kid?"

The couple exchanged a glance. Leslie spoke first. "Ariel mentioned him a few times. They were in the same treatment program before she came to us."

"February of this year, you said?"

She nodded. "What is this all about, Detective?"

Ryan took a long slug of coffee. "I hate the one to have to be the one telling you this, but he's dead."

Leslie gasped, bringing her hand to her mouth. Matthias put a comforting arm around his wife's shoulders. "How?"

"We're still working that out. Any reason to think your daughter might have maintained contact with this young man?"

The couple both shook their heads, staring down at

Tyler's picture.

"Okay." Ryan nodded, taking another sip of coffee. "Mind if I ask her myself? I'll leave it to you to break the news in a manner you feel fitting since you are her guardians."

If Sylviana Gomez was the heat of the sun, Ariel Petrenko was the light of the full moon. Ryan knocked on her door, and if she answered, he didn't hear it before trying the handle and opening the door. The door opened with a creak, revealing walls covered in black and blues, with paintings, posters and glitter all around. Ryan turned the corner and saw Ariel Petrenko lying on her bed, eyes closed, headphones tight to her skull. Her skin was pale. Her hair was dyed black with streaks of violet. She wore a black, long sleeved shirt bearing a band logo on the front. Black tights covered her legs. Ryan waved once, twice, then a third time to no avail. He pulled his LED flashlight out and flashed it twice in her eyes.

Ariel screamed, ripped the headphones from her ears and cowered against her pillows. "Get out of here. This is private!"

Ryan moved the light from her to his badge, then to the ground. "Easy, Ariel, I'm Detective Calder with the local police. I have a couple of questions regarding a friend of yours. Okay?"

The goth girl moved slowly from her corner.

"What local police?" she asked in a shaking voice.

"Metro PD." Ryan offered, extending his badge in her direction. "You can check it out if you don't believe me."

She shook her head. "I believe you. What do you want?"

Ryan put his badge and flashlight away. "I get these

cases from time to time where a parent really worries about something, and it winds up being nothing. I'm sure you've seen them."

Ariel smiled but didn't look at him. "Modern media."

"This kid went missing a couple of nights ago. His folks have me out knocking on doors. I'm sure he's fine, but I need to ask around, to make them happy."

Ariel shrugged her shoulders slightly, still looking away.

"I'm sure he's gonna wind up back home before I even file my report, but I need to ask some questions to tie off loose ends. If I show you a picture, Ariel, could you tell me if you've seen this kid before?"

Silence. Several breaths then several more. "Sure, Detective."

"Cool," Ryan replied, holding up Tyler's mug shot from his arrest before Greenleaf. "Seen this kid?"

Ariel looked up at the image. Her lips curled downward and tears filled the corners of her eyes. She blinked several times. A moment later, she answered. "Tyler Daniels. We were together at Greenleaf. We hung out sometimes. That was like a hundred years ago. I hardly knew him."

"Talked to him since you left, Ariel?"

"No," she said, turning her eyes to the computer streaming the music.

Ryan nodded. Liar. "Do you like it here?"

She sniffed and wiped her eyes, looking back up at him. "I guess. The Shaws are really trying hard."

"I agree. I think they really love you. I hope things work out for you here." Ryan sized up his options. He hadn't gained her trust, and there weren't any mirrors or opportunities to check her for tattoos. Ryan uploaded what he recorded to Jace. He opened his hands to present no threat. "I appreciate you answering my questions,

Ariel. I'm gonna get out of your room now, okay?"

She nodded without a sound.

Ryan recognized a few words through the earphones she had dropped to her neck. He stopped. "You like that version?"

Ariel lifted her head from her knee. "What do you mean, that version?"

The detective smiled. "This isn't original. This is a remake. Go ahead, sing it."

Ariel met his eyes and sang along to the song she worshipped. "Girl of Sixteen, whole life ahead of her, slashed her wrists, bored with life. Thank the Lord for small mercies."

Ryan nodded as Ariel continued with the lyrics. Once she finished the chorus he waved his hand in air. "Stop it."

The pale girl reached over to the remote and paused it in the middle of the instrumental bridge. Ryan looked down at her. "Girl of Eighteen, fell in love with everything, found new life in Jesus Christ. Hit by a car. Ended up on a life support machine."

She stared at him. "How did you..."

Ryan nodded. "It's a remake. Look it up. This isn't the first time this story has been told. Check out the original. I think you'll like it."

Ariel looked down. Ryan watched her as he walked back to the exit. "This isn't the first time a young woman has suffered. The story doesn't have to repeat itself. I hope you get that." He opened the door leaving her room. He looked back, but Ariel hadn't moved.

The door closed behind him in silence.

Ariel Petrenko broke into tears as the door closed. The lyrics of her solace song echoed in her head. "And when I die, I expect to find him laughing..." She had always felt God hated her, that he made her his puppet. The detective had touched a nerve with his visit.

"He has no idea," Rachnelle whispered in her ear.

Ariel wiped the tears from her eyes. "He knows. He knows about Tyler. He knows what we did."

Rachnelle wrapped around her host, calmness and control pouring into her veins. "He suspects, but he knows nothing. He is simple. Our plans are above him. You still sing with me, don't you, Ariel?"

The Goth girl fought the shaking of her hands and the trembling of her tears. "Yes...yes...I do."

Rachnelle sang to her hostess, intent on bringing confidence and calm. "Sing with me, Ariel. I do enjoy your voice mixed with mine. Sing for me."

The two female voices mixed in harmony, and they sang.

"You lead me on with those innocent eyes, you know I love the element of surprise,

In the Garden, I was playing the Tart, I kissed your lips and broke your heart.

You...you said you'd wait to the end of the world."

CHAPTER 13

She sat patiently in the snow, cross-legged, waiting. Her katana rested in her lap. It had taken months of searching, but she'd been pulled to Svear. She'd trekked a long way. She wasn't a fan of the snow and ice, but she'd dealt with it before. Where her Master went, she did too. She'd slept in the cold snow many a night. This waiting was nothing but a miniature trial.

Hours ago, she'd seen the blonde Scandinavian fall, her energy reaching out and wrapping around Shia, dragging her across the battle field to her side. She'd fought well but been overpowered by her Rus attackers. The double-edged sword she'd fought so valiantly with now lay by her side. Shia knew better than to touch another's weapon. When the woman came back into her body, she'd likely come up swinging.

She'd dispatched the men. They'd thought a demon appeared in the midst the way she'd suddenly been in front of them, katana in hand, dark hair whipping about her body standing over the fallen woman. She wasn't about to let them take off with her body as a trophy. She'd purposely worn all white to blend in with her landscape. Until she'd removed her hood, she'd been part of the snow. She knew most of them would never have seen a female such as she. They'd never traveled near the lands she came from, most never would.

They'd gone running, giving her no chance to test her sword and speed against their larger and slower weapons and forms. She'd heard them mutter words like demon and undead in their native language. No, those were the things she hunted. Apparently, she was about to have help in her long battle. She should have chased them down, instead, she'd dropped into the snow by the woman's side, duty bound to sit and wait.

Snow began to fall around her. She sincerely hoped the next time she'd sensed something like this, it was transporting her to a warmer climate, but she couldn't refuse the call. She'd been on her own too long.

She pulled her hood up again, blending back into her surroundings.

A gasp. Then, coughing. The woman before her came up in a fluid motion, her hand reaching for her sword before she even lifted her head to look around. Her blond braids swung around her as her wild blue eyes searched and landing on Shia.

She waited.

A smattering of a language came at her in rapid fire too fast for her to catch most of it. The blonde turned, searching for her attackers. One knee still down in the snow. Shia knew it was taking her a while to process the feeling in her body again. She'd been through the pain.

Again, the rapid-fire questions in a language she barely understood. She caught a few words, here or there. She'd picked up some things in her travels, but this language, coarse and guttural was strange to her tongue. She kept falling all over herself with it. She needed to be back in more civilized areas.

She slowly lifted a hand, and pointed a finger at herself, "Shia."

The woman's sword lowered. A frown appeared between her eyebrows.

"Shia." She repeated again. It was the name she'd chosen for herself when she'd woken on the battlefield, the dead littered about. Tomei Gozen had died on that field, instead, Zenshi Jin Ronin, the tender Buddhist without a home, had been born on the battlefield where so many of her people had died around her.

The blonde's eyes widened in understanding, and she pointed to her own chest, "Ilsa."

Shia nodded. It gave them a starting place. Names were names regardless of language. She glanced around, wary of having stayed out in the open for too long. She couldn't be sure that Ilsa's attackers wouldn't return, if only to loot her body. They needed to move to safer ground.

The blonde looked down at herself and saw the blood stain on her chest where the sword had pierced her straight through the heart. She tried to look back over her shoulder and down her back. When she looked back at Shia, a question in her eyes, Shia nodded.

"Ég dó?" She asked and then mimicked the sword slicing clean through her.

Shia nodded. "Yes, you died. And now, you're back. Við þurfum að fara. We need to go." She'd picked up enough of the language, enough to manage the basics. It would have been nice if she'd resurrected with the instant ability to know languages, but she still had to work at it. Thankfully, it never took long.

Ilsa started shaking her head, reseating her sword. "Engin."

No.

"Já" Shia responded. Yes, she needed to get them to

safety, hidden, before they came back and realized their dead prey was back, completely healthy and ready to fight again.

"Lady, you died, we need to move, I don't have time to argue. We wasted too much time waiting for you to recover." She stood up in a fluid motion, whipping her katana out and over, back into its place on her back. She took out her shorter blade and rolled up the sleeve of her coat, baring her forearm. With a quick motion, she sliced a deep cut across her skin, hissing at the pain.

So maybe she couldn't die, but getting hurt still, well, hurt.

The blonde gasped and darted forward as if to pull the weapon from her hand. Shia held up the dagger and pointed down at her arm. Ilsa's eyes followed the action. The blue-eyed gaze darted from her arm, where the cut healed itself at a rapid pace, back up to Shia's eyes.

She nodded her head at the blonde Scandinavian, taking the dagger to point to herself, and back at Ilsa.

Ilsa looked down at her chest and then back to Shia's arm. A frown formed. She held out her forearm. Shia stopped and tilted her head. Ilsa made a motion across her forearm, the same dagger slicing motion.

Shia's breathing hitched. She wanted proof. She nodded and held up the dagger. The blonde nodded back at her, taking a firmer stance in the snow. Her arm steady.

She sliced quick and deep, wincing at the growl of pain from the other woman. They both held their ground as they watched the deep wound mend together, heal up and disappear all together.

Blue eyes raised to hers, resolved. "Já. Við þurfum að fara."

Yes, they needed to go.

Shia nodded and replaced her dagger. Her hood pulled up around her face, blending in again with the snow. She turned, with Ilsa next to her, leading them from her death ground. The larger woman kept a steady pace with her.

Neither noticed the snow covered tracks filling in behind them until nothing was left but the even spread of snow completely covering any sign of battle, or resurrection.

The House of Ronin had welcomed one more.

CHAPTER 14

Ryan stopped and rubbed his eyes. One more image of a naked woman holding a snake and an apple and he might go completely insane. Over two hours of searching, and the most concrete evidence of Lilith in modern times was her tie-ins to sci-fi villains, costume designs for her in various video games, pictures from the San Diego Comic-Con, and adult fantasy videos. He'd gone looking for a legendary evil and wound up in a virtual porn shop. The results were nothing more than a diluted caricature of whatever Lilith might have been.

The endless stream of sources made his head hurt. Lilith appeared in Jewish mythology, the Babylonian Talmud, and Mesopotamian texts, and a string of modern day sci-fi novels fueled by the growing craze for vampires, werewolves, zombies, and all things supernatural. She was listed as everything from the first wife of Adam to the mother of modern telepaths. Ryan slugged down the rest of his coffee and changed the search criteria to eliminate science fiction and fantasy.

The tired detective tried to figure out what resource he could use for research. Shia was busy. Father Munoz? No, with one mention of a possible alternative to Adam and Eve, the priest would shut Ryan down before he even opened his mouth. Who else was left?

"Jace, I need you to loan me an assist here."

"Pardon me, Detective?"

"I have to toss a theory up against a spider web of logic loops. You got that in you?"

"Logical deductive theory is my specialty. What did you have in mind?"

"I have a mythical figure and a scared teenager. Shall we start there?" Ryan asked the AI.

"Speak your mind, Detective. I'll do what I can to eliminate rogue theories and suspects."

Ryan drew in a deep breath and exhaled. He focused. Eliminate conjecture and offer proven fact. "Okay, Jace, here's what I have. Recall all the facts about the deaths of Tyler Daniels, Sapphire Blade, or whatever her real name might be, and her kill, Mason Cofield. I need a diagram displaying any connections."

"Any other potential logical connections, Detective?"

Ryan shook his head. "Not yet, Jace, run this and get me a list of names." He wanted some form of steady ground to start on. Biological evidence, interrogation, and science were his comfort zone. This supernatural shit was still brand new to him. He silently hoped Shia was having better results with her investigation. He grabbed his coat, leaving his desk at the precinct and heading out. Checking in on Shia was exactly what he needed.

"Jace?" Shia asked as she stepped into her office at the warehouse, steaming mug of tea in hand.

"Yes, Lady Ronin."

She curled her feet under her in her chair, eyes scanning the screens before her. She'd finally found time to rest, and her brain engaged once again. "Report."

"Detective Ryan has been out and about following leads associated to Tyler Daniels. He asked me to run connections on the two homicides you have agreed are connected, but unsure how." He stated.

She nodded, "Turn the back wall into a crime board, start putting the connections up."

The back wall shimmered, pictures and statistics appearing on the board. The light in the office muted so the images appeared sharper, more refined.

First column, Tyler Daniels. The second, Mason Cofield and Sera Ann Nicholsen aka Sapphire Blade. The only current connection for all of them, the markings, matching heart shaped images on the base of all victim's necks appeared in the final column. On another portion of the wall, the Washington DC map blinked into being, dots marking the location of the murders. In another corner, details flowed up on the Lilin and Lilith. They'd narrowed down their demonic influence to the succubi clan. Her only problem now, how to catch the creature.

"Has Ryan uploaded his information on the connections to Tyler Daniels?" She asked, frowning at the wall. "And, do a quick scan to Virginia and Maryland reports. Let's make sure our demon is staying within the District and not roaming any further."

"All confirmed to be within the District. No images showing the heart shaped marking appearing in any open homicide cases in any jurisdiction other than our own."

She breathed a sigh of relief. Thankfully, most demons preferred to mark out a territory and remain within it. It made life much easier for her.

The screen beside her rang, and she cast a glance out of the corner of her eye.

"Speaker, Jace." She said. Her sister's visage filled the screen. "How can I help you, Ilsa?"

"I'm looking over this business proposal that showed up on my desk out of nowhere." The woman said.

Shia nodded, her eyes still trained on her crime wall, looking for patterns, nuances. "You'll like it. Should provide us unlimited funding, so long as Jace and I keep creating."

"You would step down from your role as Chief Medical Examiner for Metro PD?" Ilsa asked.

Shia's head snapped around to stare at her sister. "What?"

"To do this all, you would leave your current role, wouldn't you?" She asked.

"No." Shia's eyebrows forked down, her jaw set. "You'll see in the file. We've outlined what roles are needed for the organization. You have more than enough of our inventions to get them started before you even need anything more from us. Put Celeste in charge as the face of the company if you want. She's got the power in her to take it global. Plus, I'm sure she'd love the challenge. And, at the rate we've been adding sisters in the last hundred years, I'm sure we'll have someone soon to send her way to help her keep the streets safe."

Ilsa was already nodding in agreement. "You're right, both on the timelines and the focus. She's bored where she is now; Europe is quiet for the moment. The vamps are infighting. This would be the perfect challenge for her. Right now, she's also well known enough to make an impact with it. We'll have to setup a path to replace her and resurrect her as time goes on."

Shia nodded. At the moment, the Parisian socialite would bring a certain power and elegance to the tech company she'd proposed, leaving her to continue to focus on what she did best, hunting and killing demons. Besides, Celeste's domain had been relatively quiet for a while European economic downfall and all, she'd love a way to keep busy on a daily basis. It wasn't as if the woman hadn't held sway and made history in France in the past. She could certainly do so even more now.

"You need any help with the current issue?" Ilsa asked.

"Not unless you have information on the Lilin or Lilith you haven't uploaded to the database." Shia sighed.

She could see Ilsa shake her head. "No, it's all there. The others are fairly busy, except Celeste. Taji tracked Shellie down in the Sierra Nevada's. She has her hands full trying to heal the child who the Rissu hauled off and something about a shifter who'd been hurt as well going after the Rissu. I'm not quite sure I understand any of it, but they both reported in and are safe and not requesting aid."

Shia turned back to the screen. "How are the rest?"

"Raisa's returned to LA, apparently having issues with a stuntman there who seems immune to injury. He crashed into a solid wall and walked away. And some sort of shadow demon she can't name yet. She hasn't asked for help, so things are going smoothly, or as smoothly as they can for the Rus."

Shia knew the woman still had issues they'd saved one of those kind who'd first killed her.

Ilsa's gaze strayed, probably to one of her other screens. "We're having as many issues with the human men as the demons."

Shia nodded well aware of her own situations with a certain sexy detective. She didn't fault her sisters for these sudden issues with the male species. She didn't understand it herself. She allowed herself a brief moment of seeing him in her mind's eye before focusing on the data streaming in a small window next to Ilsa's face on screen. She scanned it quickly.

Aureline was tangled up with poachers and some sort of lion demon from the Neo-Sumerian age. Shellie in the Sierra Nevada's healing an injured child and some shifter male. She'd decided to stay with the child until she was better healed to travel. Shia had a feeling the shifter played a large part in her decision as well. Yvaine tangling with a group of fledgling vampires in Russia. Her report mentioned something about a musician she'd been protecting as well. Iniko was stuck, and frustrated, hunting down a tribe of Biloko. Shia shuddered at the thought of the dwarf like creatures with their sharp claws and snouts full of teeth ready to eat people. Taji returning home. Christelle hunted the waterless spaces in Australia, and Maya back to playing in the shadows of the elite in Saudi Arabia.

"Looks like everyone is working at full capacity." Shia nodded. "Let me know if any of them need reinforcements. We can reallocate Christelle and Maya if need be. Iniko might need help and maybe Yvaine. I don't like that they're dealing with packs not singles, especially since they have so little experience."

"I'll wait until they request backup then and keep an eye on those two. If need be, I'll follow Yvaine and send Maya to back Iniko before returning to rub elbows with the oil barons." Ilsa turned away from the screen. Shia could hear the sounds of the clicking of keys across the Net.

Ryan heard Shia speaking with another woman as he entered the room. He stopped in his tracks, looking at the changes to office, more importantly, the images along the back wall. He recognized scenes from their current case file, publicity shots, headshots, and more, each with notes underneath. "Nice work. Some of the dinosaurs in the office still print those out and do everything on pen and paper."

Shia smiled over at him, clicking her connection to the screen nearest her off. "Yes, we're going to work on bringing them into this age. You can use your fingertips to rearrange things too if you'd like or ask Jace to. We were trying to build the connections." She made a mental note to make the new company give a technical grant as a pilot to the Metro PD, at least then, she wouldn't have to be doing as much work as she had been.

She stood up and walked over to the wall. "I'm still basing most of my research off Tyler as the first kill and the most important. What drew the Lilin here was a powerful need and the way Tyler died implied a personal connection. The others only bare a passing connection and not nearly as gruesome."

"The girls, you mean. I had Jace craft me a list. Not many results, to tell you the truth." Ryan walked over to stand next to her. He looked down briefly, water drops littering around his body. "I'm dripping on your floor. I hope you don't mind." He gestured at the snow melting on his coat.

"Jace will have that cleaned up in no time." She cut him a glance, gaze trailing over him. "Do you need to clean up? Warm up before we work on the report from the girls?" She asked, a frown marring her brow. "There's spare rooms upstairs, a shower or the sauna. And I'm sure," She cast a glance at the screen on her desk. "There will be a clean set of clothes before you're done with it all."

Ryan looked at her while she watched the computer. The first response in his head involved her and a hot shower and quickly morphed into ideas for the sauna. He shook his head. People were dying. Everything else could wait. It had to. "Jace's list included eight girls who shared a facility with Tyler. Two of them are dead. The Bailess twin sisters are right out. They would put Tyler on a pedestal. They're fanatics, not killers. Nicole Partridge is a deaf/mute. That leaves three more."

"Jace, put 'em up." Ryan ran a hand through his wet hair while images of Sylviana Gomez, Ariel Petrenko and Eclipse appeared on the crime board. "I suppose all three are capable. Gomez is a short-fused graffiti artist. She's definitely got the anger issues. Eclipse was nowhere to be found. She runs away weekly, so she's got the attachment issues market cornered. Petrenko doesn't have...I don't know what she has. She's...what's the right word?" Ryan thought. Sad was too vague. "You ever been to Cape Cod, Shia?"

Shia looked startled as she turned her head to look at him, she'd been so focused on the images of the girls faces as they'd appeared on screen. "Cape Cod? Perhaps, maybe in passing."

He realized she'd probably been so many places that the memories blurred together. "There's a famous landmark in Cape Cod. Ever heard of Guglielmo Marconi?"

She shook her head even as Jace put up a picture on the screen before them.

Ryan looked at the image of Marconi's Wellfleet Beach monument. "Yeah, yeah, Jace. Can I? I can touch this, right?"

"Of course, sir. Touchscreens are all the rage right now. This entire office, every surface can be used as a touch screen. Even the desks and the floor if need be." Jace answered.

Ryan raised his eyebrows. "That's pretty damn cool." He regained his composure and then apparently had a thought. "Jace, if you ever do that to my car, I'll kill you."

"Of course not sir, Lady Shia has issued a command that I can no longer make modifications to your car without your permission or your request." The AI commented.

He smiled at Shia, who apparently, from the way she'd focused on the images, didn't appreciate the sidebar conversation. Ryan tapped the image of Marconi station. "Okay, in 1901, Marconi sent the first wireless communication across the Atlantic Ocean. He did it from this location on Cape Cod." Ryan turned the image so it became an aerial view. "There was a central building and four large towers with concrete bases used to generate the signal. That was over a century ago."

She nodded. "I remember the news now. It set the world on fire."

He paused, nodding slowly. "Right. Jace, pull up a geological horizon mapping of the beach now."

The AI obeyed, adding another image to the touch screen. Ryan turned the original, making it a horizontal view. Then he slid the second image over the first. The differences were obvious. Three of the towers and the building were gone, fallen into the ocean. Most of what remained was a tribute to Marconi's achievement, not the original structures.

"See this," he continued, putting his hands on the screen to accent the original and what was left. The space between his hands showed everything that had crumbled away. "This, all this, all this that has eroded away." He met Shia's eyes. "That's Ariel Petrenko."

Shia stilled as she looked up at the screen, looking as if she was taking it all in. "Then, she's our girl. Regardless, that you haven't spoken to the one called Eclipse. Those who call to a succubus are broken, hurt, wounded and not headstrong and capable of ticking most people off. We need her records, data, grades, friends. Anything we can find about her and how she pulled the Lilin to her."

Ryan nodded. Finding information in the social system wasn't easy, and it wasn't all in digital format. He'd have to do some legwork and pull some strings to get everything he could. He still struggled with the thought that the young, pained girl he had spoken to a few hours ago could bring about death.

"Jesus, Shia, what could Tyler Daniels have done to her that made her..."

"Detective, Lady Shia, incoming calls to both your phones." Jace interrupted.

Shia glanced at her phone. "Trouble." She picked it up and turned away, taking the call to her ear.

Ryan grabbed his phone the moment it vibrated, staring at Shia's back, his question still hanging in the air. "Calder."

CHAPTER 15

It burned, oh how it burned. Pain, fire, and heat ripped through her. She coughed, spasms racing through her body. She tried, so very hard, not to cry out, but the pain, exquisite in its focus forced it out of her. By all that was, it hurt.

She rolled over onto her back, not even flinching as she landed on the hand of someone else, someone unmoving. She'd fallen on the battle field often enough to know very few counted among the living. She tried to take a deep breath and succeeded only in making herself cough again. The pain swept over her.

She counted, over and over again, recited battle plans, whatever she could do as she her body began to repair itself. Fast, this was too fast. She shouldn't feel her bones mending, the skin pulling itself back together. But she swore she could, and it hurt.

It hurt.

She groaned, knowing better, but unable to stop herself.

Their enemy likely swept the battlefield searching for survivors to either take into trade, if they lived, or slice their throats open. Being female, she knew she'd be taken into trade. The men, they'd slit their throats, raid their weapons and move on. She wasn't about to let that happen.

Her bones shifted, and the pain lessened in her lungs. Her ribs fell back into place. She groaned again and then stilled, focusing on her hearing.

Footsteps, shouts, all drawing too close for comfort.

She forced her eyes open. Darkness, the black of night. Stars twinkled overhead. She turned her head and saw the light of torches bobbing and weaving across the battlefield. She needed to move, gone before they drew too near.

She took a deep breath in and willed her body to cooperate with her. She was unique among her kind, female samurai, battle trained. She'd fought alongside her mentor, her master for many years, trained from birth to be more than a woman, to be the ultimate weapon.

She would not be taken by enemy forces, even if she couldn't explain how she'd survived the death strike she'd taken, a katana straight through her heart. She'd worry about the why of it all later, right now, she needed to move and move fast.

Her eyes adjusted even further to the night, and she forced herself to her feet, moving as slowly as she could while taking stock of her situation.

Men coming, combing the dead on the field. The forest to her back. Her only chance of survival, even as the temperature continued to drop. The forest it would be. She began to step backwards through the dead bodies. She should stop to gather supplies, take what she could, but the coming men pushed her to move faster than she should.

Her foot hit something, a loud clang echoed across the field.

"Aho." She thought, but her mouth remained shut.

She was an idiot fledgling. She knew better, knew how to walk quietly in the most silent spaces.

She turned and darted through the darkness, no longer trying to keep quiet, but her feet fell exactly where they needed to. She reached the tree line as an arrow pierced the tree next to her. She never stopped, darting deeper into the forest, far away from the battle.

A few miles in, her pace finally slowed, her breathing unlabored. She stopped at the base of a massive tree and took stock. Her weapons? Check, still firmly in place, her katana on her back, her knives and her throwing stars. She'd lost her bow and arrows. She sighed. Those would have to be replaced. She would find the wood to recreate them, a better set. One pouch of water. She could replenish that easily in these woods. Her horse? Long gone. Food, new issue.

She was quite certain she couldn't return to the palace now. Her master had released her before dying on the battlefield. He'd commanded she leave him. Something he'd never done. Then, she'd seen him fall and gone on a rampage herself, grabbing the sword of a dead mate and using it along with her own to hack through the battle. She'd taken out quite a few, no small feat for her size and stature.

So, she was on foot and needed food. Both things she could handle.

It was then the hairs on the back of her neck stood up. She turned her head ever so slightly, a deep guttural growl flowed over her. Eyes of the deepest red glowed at her in the night. Black on black fur. She counted, four paws, if this was a dog, it was the largest dog she'd ever seen. It easily stood as tall as she, on four feet. She'd hate to see its reach on two.

Her katana slid from her scabbard before she even recognized she'd reached for it. A foul odor emanated from the creature. She wrinkled her nose and then forced herself to ignore it.

Dog? No, unlike any dog she'd ever encountered. Its glowing red eyes sent her heartbeat into overdrive.

Out of the fire and...into something else entirely.

The beast growled at her again. She turned, facing it completely. Her sword twirled in her hand. She wished, briefly, for her bow and arrows, sure she could have taken out the beast before it could think to move. Bad for her that she had only her bladed weapons. A mist began to form under their feet. She flicked a glance at it, before quickly returning her gaze to the dog.

Unseemly.

She'd died. She had to have. No one survived a sword piercing their heart the way she had. She'd understood it while it happened. She'd processed it. And now, she'd left the real world and entered some level of hell. She had no other explanation. She knew reality, the harsh training, the hell of a life. And, she'd been educated in the stories of the other realms, never believing in them, but always having a healthy respect for the lessons they taught.

And now, she was face to nose with one of them.

The hellhound growled at her again, one large paw toyed with the ground beneath it. Mist exploded in small puffs around it.

Large, yes. Evil, oh definitely. Completely focused on her? Yes.

Could her day get any better?

"Bring it, puppy. I've already died once today." She twirled the sword. Yes, she'd died, and something had brought her back on the field of battle. Was it for this? Had she lost one master only to wake to serve another?

The hellhounds eyes never swayed from hers.

He lifted his lip in a snarl. She dropped into a crouch,

ready to move in whatever direction she needed to, her sword held ready.

He leapt, but away from her, darting through the woods leaving a trail of red haze drifting behind him.

She stood up, her katana slowly lowering.

What the...?

She rested her head against the trunk of the tree she perched in. She'd been holed up here for hours, waiting. In the three days since she'd run into the hellhound in the middle of her forest, the inhuman creature had killed four people and injured several more. She hadn't realized what it was, until she'd heard the whisperings in town and followed its ever glowing red trail.

She'd lost the trail at the creek. The demon creature was smarter than any normal dog she'd ever met.

She'd figured out its pattern, mostly. Thus she was in this tree, hoping she'd catch it before it headed out for its next meal. The red mist preceded it this time. Its eyes glowed in the dark, eerie, red. Its black fur looked more leather than fur like. His ears tufted out, angled on its head. Long, deadly claws slashed the ground as it wound its way around the forest floor.

Shia silently notched an arrow. She'd had the time to re-craft her bow and several arrows, a finer quality than the last and more lovingly made. These ones held the power of her own hands rather than those given to her. She'd had nothing but time and focused her time on using every bit of her knowledge to pour energy and power into her weapons.

She waited, then waited, and then let it fly.

The arrow lodged itself in a glowing eye.

The resulting growl reverberated through the forest.

The beast continued to move forward. Shia shimmed down the tree to the forest floor frowning when her next arrow simply bounced off the creature's hide. She drew her sword as her feet touched down. The katana light in her hand as she twirled it around. This time there would be no walking away.

The creature's long fangs snapped closed, and its one good eye targeted completely on her. It lowered its head to the ground and reached over to snap the arrow from its eye.

"Smart, powerful. How did you come into being, beast?" Shia asked it. She knew it couldn't provide an answer.

The creature stood its ground, growling at her. She waited, wanting it to make the first move. She watched its muscles ripple under the leathery skin. She couldn't call it fur really, although it tufted here and there like fur. Its tail swished back and forth as it watched her.

She shivered slightly under the red gaze. The creature was something more powerful than the foes she'd faced on the battlefield. No man had fought with such a creature as this. At least none that she knew. The men had talked around the campfires some nights, of creatures of the night, things of legends. One of those legends stood before her, deciding how to kill her.

Problem was, she couldn't die. Pain? Yes. Suffering? Yes. She knew all of that now, and she knew it had to die. It couldn't be left to roam these woods.

It began to slowly circle her. Shia moved as it did, circling back. When the hellhound tensed its back claws digging further into the earth, she shifted her stance, preparing to take the hit full on. At the last moment, she slid sideways, katana singing through the air, slicing with full force through the beast's neck.

The thousand-year-old sword severed the head of the

beast in a single motion.

Shia dropped to one knee, heart pounding. The blade of her sword tipped down, allowing her to rest against it as the hellhounds body dropped to the ground, the head rolling to the side of it. She watched, unmoving as it shattered into millions of pieces of black dust, falling to the ground. The red haze melted into the earth around it. A scorched pattern the only sign the beast had been there to begin with.

Shia stood, returning her sword to its sheath. There would be no more deaths attributed to that one. Her first otherworldly kill. A sense of satisfaction welled up within her. She'd thought she roamed without purpose and reason. She thought she'd died serving her master. She had both now, a new purpose and a new master.

She closed her eyes and lifted her chin to the sky breathing and reaching out to sense which direction she needed to travel next. The faint tugging from behind her had her turning. When the pull became stronger, more insistent, she opened her eyes and started to jog through the night. Apparently, her new master wished to remain hidden, giving her only glimpses of energy.

For a brief moment, she wondered what her next target would be. Then she pushed the thought from her head. No worries, just her next mission.

She smiled at herself, who'd have thought it? Female demon hunting samurai.

CHAPTER 16

Pranati Sharma sighed. Managing her boss's calendar alone was a full time job. Running errands, screening calls, and mastering office politics took up plenty of time. She wasn't certain where her job ended and where her life began. She managed to squeeze in the fairly anonymous social media cry for help, and she smiled as her former classmates commiserated. Pranati had come over on her student visa; the first of her family to attend college, and last spring, the first of her family to graduate. She immediately posted local ads looking for an internship. Within two weeks, she had earned a summer intern position in her field of veterinary science. Once that ended, she applied to every ad in the classifieds.

She nearly panicked when she was asked to interview at Bryant & Meinrad. The law firm represented many of the highly recognized intellectual property lawsuits brought against the Federal government. Still, here she was, two months later, holding down a full-time, salaried position as the executive assistant to Kyle Bryant. Kyle, great-grandson to the firm's founding father, focused largely on patent infringement. He was a legal superstar, in his early thirties, complete with vacation homes in

Europe, limousines, helicopters, and a practical army of call girls at his disposal.

Pranati smiled and licked her lips. He was the perfect fuel for her fire. A few years ago, she had escaped the region of Bihar, India, empowered by her family's life savings. She fled India the moment she had been accepted on a student visa, and her every breath carried the hopes of her family. She had taken side jobs in tutoring, fast food, and retail, sending every extra penny to her family as she earned her degree. Once her studies concluded, she was caught without a future, without direction. She was desperate for a path to success. She put out a call to the universe.

Pranati rubbed her neck, wincing at the scabbing of the fresh tattoo beneath her fingertips. The pain brought a smile to her face. Kyle Bryant had never asked her into his office alone before. Still, the light flashed on her phone, indicating his page. Pranati smiled and pushed the button to answer the summoning of her latest master.

"You called for me?"

"Sit down, Miss Sharma."

Pranati closed the heavy Mahogany doors behind her. "As you wish, sir."

Her Kelsi Dagger heels clicked loudly against the marble floor as she approached the pair of patent leather chairs that faced her boss's desk.

She reached the closest chair and stopped.

"Wait," Kyle Bryant whispered, his eyes prowling her body.

Pranati paused. "You summoned me, sir."

"Yes, yes I did."

"Is there somewhere else you would prefer I sit?" She lifted her eyes to meet his. The lust was tangible.

Kyle smiled. "So glad you asked. As a matter of fact, I have the perfect spot for you. How about you come around to my side of the desk, Miss Sharma?"

The olive-skinned secretary stopped for a moment, as their eyes locked. "I would love to come to you, Mister Bryant."

The lawyer chuckled. "Mister Bryant was my old man's old man. The rich old man who is still paying the bills." She moved closer, and he wrapped an arm around her waist. "You can just call me 'I'm coming', or 'Oh, God, fuck me harder'. Either one works for me."

Pranati smiled, hiking up her skirt and straddling his lap. His erection was evident, even beneath his expensive suit. "Do you think you have what it takes to make me climax?"

Kyle fed on her movement like an addict. "You bet your ass I do."

The lithe woman smiled. "I'll take that bet, and your life along with it."

Ryan whipped the Impala through traffic to the corner of 12th and Massachusetts. The first responders and black and whites were all over the place. A large crowd gathered outside of the police perimeter, and he struggled to find a path that wouldn't bump into a reporting camera crew. "They're going to want some answers. I'll distract them. You get upstairs and find out what the hell happened to these two, fair?"

"Fair. I'll wait till you have them focused elsewhere before I leave the vehicle. Jace, scramble all video for the moment. Cause a hiccup the minute I leave the car." Shia replied.

"Yes ma'am." The AI said.

A look of annoyance crossed her face before disappearing under a smooth mask of calm.

Ryan armed the car as he exited. He took a look around and scoffed. The DC Campaign to Prevent Teen Pregnancy's headquarters butted up the crime scene. Lovely. It took a few seconds for the wind to bite at his skin. It took only a few more for the media to notice him and head his way.

"Detective! Detective!" came the calls. He hadn't prepared a statement. These bobbleheads were going to be disappointed.

"Ryan!"

He looked over his shoulder, meeting a familiar, confident smile. "Chris Weitzel, from The Washington Insider, can you tell us what you know about the murder victims?"

Only he heard the faint click of the door opening and closing as Shia exited the car. He sensed her more than heard her as she made a quick path across the scene.

He looked at the Insider's most famous, new, reporter, the young man who had cracked the Spiros case and subsequent fatal plane accident. Ryan put on his best fake smile. "I can't confirm anything, Mr. Weitzel. You folks haven't let me upstairs to get any information."

"Are you confirming there are multiple homicide victims, Detective?"

"I can't confirm anything while I'm standing here, posing for your headlines. Let me do my job, and the department will issue a statement as soon as we have something to report."

Weitzel pretended to stumble, falling close enough that Ryan had to catch him, or let him eat wet slush. Ryan stepped back. Weitzel pushed himself up to his feet, looking indignantly at the other reporters for whoever had allegedly pushed him to the ground. He smiled up at Ryan. "What can a guy do for an inside scoop, Detective?"

Ryan patted the young man on his wet head. "Watch your step, kid."

He snapped "no comment" several more times as he made his way through the media swarm and crossed the police tape. Patrick O'Shaughnessy met him at the threshold.

"Any instructions, Detective?" The older man asked.

"Yeah," Ryan huffed, his breath steaming in the air. "If they get pushy, call in the SWAT team. And, O'Sho..."

"Yeah?"

"If you use tear gas, aim for the blonde kid with the Nikon."

Shia leaned over the body of the female victim. No marks. Nothing but the mark of a heart at the base of her neck. If she did an autopsy, she'd bet it would prove cardiac arrest, like the last crime scene.

She sighed under her breath and moved over to the male.

Claw marks riddled his throat and body. She sighed again and snapped pictures, knowing full well she wasn't going to get any DNA or anything to help her in closing this case in the normal way.

Damn succubi clan for making it much harder for her to do her job and keep the other world hidden.

"Whoa, ouch," Ryan muttered from beside the mahogany doorframe.

Shia didn't even turn her head. "This demon...is a bitch."

"Yeah, no guy should ever have to lose his, never mind." Ryan looked at the woman's body on the floor.

"Can you determine time of death?"

"He's still warm. She's not." Shia glanced around the scene; a faint orange glow hovered around the woman's body and then, flowed off through the office building. She scowled.

"That would work if the woman had been dead longer. Which means either a third party came in, killed her, made him watch and then killed him, or..."

Shia glanced around as if to make sure it was only the two of them in listening distance, "Or, yes. Lilin, same MO but right now, I can still see a faint trail of orange heading through the office. I don't have a way to excuse myself to follow it."

"Dr. Ronin," Ryan snapped, loud enough for the other forensics team to hear him in the hallway. "We need a rape kit. There's a possible sexual assault angle here. Do you have one nearby?"

"Sorry sir, it's not in my kit. I'll have to go get it. Can your team continue with the video of the scene and gathering of evidence? I'll be right back after I get it from my vehicle." She said as she cut him a glance.

Ryan nodded. "I'll have them bag and tag what they can. I need the blood spatter guy in here to confirm a few things. Get what you need, but make it quick, Dr. Ronin. The first 48 hours are the most important. Even you lab geeks know that, right?" He winked at her as he tilted his head to counter his aggressive tone.

Shia tilted her head back at him, staring, unnerving in her unblinking gaze, "Crystal clear, Detective. Be right back."

Shia darted, knowing she had a limited time. The damn succubus was fast, faster than she'd expected, but she'd caught a hint of the demon's trail and everything in her demanded she follow it, down, through the stairwell, across the lobby floor and out the front doors, and then nothing.

It dissipated. Gone. With the wind.

She bit back a cry of annoyance. Why were the female demons such a pain to hunt down? Her teeth locked as she strode back to the Impala, under the radar, hidden right before the cameras, knowing full well not only had Jace messed with their feeds, but her internal chemical makeup did as well. She'd learned long ago. Raisa and Celeste could appear on screen, but the rest of them could not. Shia, herself, never appeared, as if her image erased itself the minute someone tried to capture her.

"Jace, rape kit." She said as she leaned into the car, knowing full well the AI had made more modifications to the Detective's car than either one of them had approved.

The passenger seat shifted open and one rape kit rose up to rest on the seat. She snagged it muttering, "Find me the pinpoints in the North West. That's the direction the energetic pattern went before I lost it. Make the connections."

She strode back into the building and up to her crime scene, seriously ticked off. Damn good thing she had an AI to go off and research while she worked. She'd keep from erasing him for all his indiscretions if he found her a link to it all.

"...which means he died right here in his chair. There's no real pattern to the lacerations, but notice the impact patterns. These are clearly medium to high-impact projected bloodstains. My guess would be a crime of passion. Maybe he said something wrong in the middle of things?" The forensic specialist stopped, eyeing the detective.

Ryan nodded. "Well, we'll confirm that with the rape kit. Good work, Seneca."

The man in scrubs and latex gloves nodded, taking his photos and his blood tests with him. He moved aside to allow Shia back into the crime scene.

"Thank you, Seneca. Get those results uploaded as soon as you can, please." She said.

She moved closer to the victim. "Rape kit as requested, Detective."

"Dollars to donuts says they had intercourse. You'll be able to tell me if it was consensual and if they used contraception, I'm sure. No one has moved her body at all, so I don't know if there's anything else that will fill us in."

"Detective, the lacerations to the male victim indicate that no, this was NOT consensual. Those were fingernail based. I can tell that without a lab study." She leaned into her female victim and swabbed her, already knowing what she was going to find when she ran the tests. "I will have to run the tests, but based on what I'm seeing, the DNA is going to link right back to him." She pointed to the dead man.

Ryan pushed the door as closed as he could without making a scene. He stormed over to her. "I know that. You know that. But this woman was hardly more than a hundred pounds soaking wet. Unless she strapped scalpels to her fingers, or suddenly summoned Freddy fucking Kruger, she couldn't do this. How do I explain this to the squad, or the media sharks circling a few floors below?"

"Ryan," she hissed. "I am making it so you can. My job is to fix this, cover it up and make it real. I'm giving you an out."

Out loud, Shia leaned back, "I'll have the rape kit

processed in a few hours, but my preliminary response, which is rarely wrong, is this got out of hand in the worst way. He forced her, she slashed him and then, she couldn't handle it...the panic overrode her heart. It just stopped."

Ryan walked to the far end of the room. Two heavy mahogany bookshelves met him, filled with volumes upon volumes of US Civil Codes. He stared for several long moments, then bowed his head. His fist curled before he realized he was doing so. With a growl, he punched the wall once, twice, then a third time before leaning stopping to pull his hand back and lean his forehead against the tomes of legal code.

"Jace, erase that from the video. Now." Shia commanded. "Shield now, repeat something."

"Detective. Ryan." She stripped off her gloves and dropped them near her victims, striding over to him. She laid a hand on his back.

He didn't flinch. "I'm a detective, Shia. I look for trends. I find the pattern. Then I unravel it, and I find where it started. It's like penciling in a kids' maze backwards."

Her sigh wrapped around him, "It's more now. I wish...I wish I could explain it, but I can't. I have no idea, no reason, no why as to why you can see, hear, or even sense any of this. In my realm, the thousands of years I've been alive, you have to be female and die in the line of battle. You're neither."

Ryan turned, but didn't face her. He listened to her words. "Tell me something."

"Tell you what?" She asked since he didn't see her nod.

"When you look back at it all. All of it, who's the first person who was special to you that you remember losing?" His voice felt raspy as he asked, and he still didn't lift his eyes from the floor.

She didn't hesitate, "The four-year-old girl who died, in the claws of the hellhound I let go because I didn't understand who or what I was when I came to on the battlefield where I'd died."

Ryan closed his eyes. "What was her name?"

"I have no idea. I don't know the names of those whom I'm called to protect, to save. I don't know her name." Shia said. "Some days, I don't know my own."

"I'll ask Father Munoz to pray for her next time I talk to him," he said, and he meant it. "What about your family?"

"Don't." She stepped back. "The child is long gone. Resurrected and still in my power to keep tabs on. My family?" She stopped. "The originals are long gone, leaving me to life of service. Now? My sisters all fight, hunt, function within the Code. None of this is important to this case."

Ryan finally raised his gaze to meet hers, his eyes full of tears. "The fuck it isn't, Shia. My job as a detective is to find patterns, trends, the answer to the riddle. What do we have? We have a killer on the loose. According to you, and I believe you, a supernatural killer. What's the pattern? Age of the victims? All over the road. Cause of death? Close. The only consistent is the possessed woman who eventually kills and then drops dead after the event. Let's profile her, shall we?"

Ryan continued, clenching his teeth. "Late twenties to early thirties, dark hair, has strong family ties, lives in or near DC." His voice trailed off, and he turned away.

"Stop." Shia said. "It's the haunted one, no one else could call a Lilin. I don't want it to be so, I hate when the young ones call something into being without understanding the results." She lifted her head up. "My job is to fix this. Find a path, make a plan and make it real. I have to find a way to fix this."

Ryan shook his head, angry. He took a breath and stared at her. "When I wake up from my nightmares, Shia, I don't see you as the one harboring this thing. I see someone else. I see someone who was hurt. I see someone strong, but flawed, and dealing with it the same way you see me. I see CC. I see my sister."

The next few hours went by in normal whirlwind fashion. Uniforms and technicians came and left, photographing, bagging up evidence, eventually bagging up the two victims. By the time it was over, Shia had a large catalog of technical and biological analysis information. Ryan was coordinating the statements gathered by the officers after commandeering one of the company's conference rooms. The information was transferred to Metro PD (and to Jace) and all that was left was to do was to notify the next of kin.

Ryan reached the Impala and the exhaustion sank into every muscle. Shia waited in the passenger seat. Her eyes darted over images and statistics with inhuman speed. He opted not to interrupt her and put the car in gear. It was slow going at first. The onlookers had mostly departed, but there was still plenty of vehicle and pedestrian traffic in DC.

They drove for half an hour in silence. Ryan didn't even turn on the radio. The outside city noise and the digital chirping of Shia's data was all there was to hear. He turned a dozen thoughts over in his head, trying to reach out to her, but they all made him feel him like a Neanderthal. He focused on driving instead. Thinking of the case just made him angry. It was unprofessional, and it wasn't helping.

Shia closed her hands, and the digital data disappeared

from view. She closed her eyes, drew in a deep breath and then slowly exhaled. Apparently, she was also clearing her mental slate. For someone with a thousand years of memories, she was astonishingly able to center and gain clarity. Maybe she could teach him before he went crazy.

He felt her gaze on him. He stole a quick sideways glance back at her. She was beautiful. She was perfect, and he was positive he would find a way to drive her away somehow. It was his track record. She opened her mouth to speak and stopped when both of their phones beckoned.

Ryan raised a finger to his lips and put the call on the car's speakers. "Calder."

"Detective, this is dispatch. There has been a double homicide reported. Officers are on scene now. 19th Street and Corcoran Street."

Ryan downshifted and pulled the Impala hard to the left, driving into a small side street. He flipped on the car's blue lights and siren. "I'm on my way."

Apparently, it was going to be one of those kinds of nights.

Shia received and answered a similar call, hoping the roaring engine and skidding tires weren't audible in the background. She could downplay the siren. They were audible almost every moment of life in DC. She prepared herself for the crime scene, calling orders to Jace to track and record everything when they arrived. "Am I going to have to have him erase all trace of your car from the street cameras, also?"

"Huh," Ryan answered, "why would you do that?"

"Disciplinary action," she replied calmly.

"Disci-what? Is that code for something?"

She sighed. "No, I understand even those on the force

have to be within reasonable limits when responding to calls. Wasn't there an officer disciplined for speeding this year?"

Ryan watched traffic from the side streets as he plowed ahead. "That was some moron rookie. He was doing 90 in a frickin' school zone. We're nowhere close to that, thank you."

She kept her eyes on him. "Jace, go ahead and erase this vehicle from camera feeds, as well."

Ryan scowled but concentrated on driving. "Saving my job?"

She smiled. "No, I don't want the two of us being pulled over for speeding. That would be hard to explain to your friends at the precinct."

He chuckled. "Always one step ahead..."

"Naturally, Detective. How else does one stay alive?"

CHAPTER 17

They pulled up to the plain condominiums as patrol officers were taping off the area in front of the building. Ryan made small talk with the uniforms outside while Shia ducked into the building. An officer was guarding the doorway to 2F while two others spoke with neighbors down the hallway. She nodded, flashing her credentials, and the officer stepped aside. She joined two techs and two EMT's as she entered.

The condo was a small, three-room model with a bedroom, kitchenette, and living room. A few steps into the room a chill ran down her spine. Her outward appearance remained calm, but she screamed a silent warning to herself.

The room smelled of burnt meat. The fan over the stovetop droned on high. The shelves had been emptied. There was no sign of smoke or fire damage in the larger room. Shia stopped to determine the origin and traced it without looking to the kitchenette. Whatever was cooking had been burned beyond being edible. Let the officers determine if that was relevant. The bodies were what mattered to her.

A male and a female, the woman lay face down on her right cheek between the kitchenette and the living room. Her face partially covered by her collar length brunette hair, but Shia could see the woman's eyes were still open and her mouth parted as if in shock. There were no apparent wounds. She made a note, hoping this was a coincidence, knowing it wasn't. A partial tattoo outline was all Shia needed to confirm. She knew Jace would build out the rest.

The man's death had been far more violent. His body lay in the kitchen, face up. Kitchen knives of various lengths protruded from his chest and stomach. His mouth had been sliced open. Two knives with shorter handles, steak knives, Shia guessed, were driven into his eyes. The amount of blood covering the floor, cabinets, and walls was hard to fathom.

Her breath caught, and her throat closed. Centuries of battle, and this was the closest thing to torture and barbarianism outside of the battlefield. She exhaled sharply, donning her gloves. She would have to go through the motions while others were present, but inside, she was on overdrive. The Lilin was growing more powerful, more violent, more raw. She and Ryan needed to get away from here quickly. The demon had to be found and dispatched.

She heard Ryan speaking to the officer in the hallway. He sounded distant, almost underwater. She shook her head to clear her thoughts. As he entered the condo, she walked to meet him. The look on her face was enough to make him stop in his tracks. She stepped closer, but not so close the others would notice. She spoke in a whisper, but her voice sounded like thunder in her head. "We need to get back to the lab as soon as possible."

The familiar scowl covered his face as he began processing what she meant. "It's her, then?"

Shia nodded silently.

He tilted his head to look past her.

"Ryan," she whispered with an edge to her voice. He met her gaze immediately.

"We have to find her. We have no time to waste. She is gaining in power."

He nodded. "She's following a pattern, like a serial killer."

"Yes, she is, and like all serial killers, the pattern has changed." Shia fought off the shudder rippling over her skin.

"She's accelerating."

Shia's fingers flew over the keyboard. Finally, two reports she could close out for the department. The crime analysis board remained lit up across the wall at her back, unsolved for her realm. She hated to do it, but it had to be done. She hit send on the email, effectively releasing the cases from all involved parties. She had to put a stop to this before the Lilin claimed another victim, because even one more death in such a manner would have them all thinking serial killer on the loose, and she'd have to medically reopen the previous two cases and start linking them together with further in depth analysis. Thankfully, Metro PD had solved a similar, easy case in between and redirected focus.

"Jace, add Ariel Petrenko's profile to the board." She stood up and snagged her katana from its resting place beside her desk. Her long flowing pants flared out around her. "I'll be in the training room taking a break."

She needed to step away from it all for a few moments alone. Down the hall to the large training room. The door slid open without a sound as she neared it.

"Jace, where is Ry...the Detective?" She asked as she stepped over the threshold. The lights came to life.

"Detective Calder is in the training hall shower at the moment." Jace answered.

Shia's imagination went into overdrive before she could stop it. The idea of Ryan's strong, lean form naked in her shower made her breathing misfire. She shook herself. No, no time to go down that road. She had no right. Instead, she walked to the weapons rack, pulling a smaller, lighter blade into her hand.

"Music, please. My workout playlist, Jace." Aural Vampire's "Human Noise" started in the speakers. The familiar sounds of her normal workout playlist filtered through hidden speakers in the room. She moved to the center of the room, rotating her wrist, getting the energy flowing.

She'd designed the room to allow her for freedom of movement. Overly large, strength training equipment lined one wall, but the majority of the space was large, open, and empty. Weapons racks lined another wall, mirrors on the far back. The hardwood floors felt at home under her bare feet.

She flipped her katana out in her right hand, the shorter wakizashi in her left. Moving in series of slow movements, she worked to warm her muscles up, energy flowing, rippling over and through her.

Basics. Using her right arm, her sword arm, she drilled her basic strikes while constantly keeping the left in a defensive position. She had mastered the fancier, showier drills, but it always came back to basic strikes. A single, correctly executed strike with her katana could take a man's head off, or a hellhound's. A smile rippled over her at the memory of it. She shook her head to focus again. The Lilin was nothing she had ever faced before.

"Jace, give me a fighting partner." Shia called out. She didn't flinch like she had the first time when the fully outfitted samurai shimmered into being before her. The hologram couldn't actually touch her, but it helped to keep her focused on a target. She'd trained so long on her own; it was nice to have even the image of an imaginary partner.

She danced out of the way when the blue sword angled a blow towards her neck. She'd spent years training with a wooden blade before her master allowed her near a bladed weapon. She had learned precision and control, complete control. She blocked another hit with the back of her blade. The hologram passed through her, had her opponent been real, human, they'd have had a beautiful ringing throughout the room.

The music went silent.

A male voiced echoed through the room. "Jace, kill this puppet show."

The hologram disappeared, she turned, and Ryan stood before her, shirtless, in a pair of black gi pants. A pair of dog tags hung around his neck. His muscled chest gleamed in the low light of the training space.

"Lady Ronin." He bowed.

She halted in mid twirl, eyes cutting his way. Sweat dripping down her throat. "You think to play swords with me, Detective?"

Ryan smirked. "Not exactly. May I have this dance, Lady Ronin?" The telescoping baton snapped to its full extension in his right hand.

Shia laughed in actual enjoyment. "Your baton against my thousand plus year old demon hunting sword? Sorry, Detective, but my blade cuts stronger than that. Would you like me to switch weapons?"

She'd never met a man so willing to play in her arena. He had to have a few screws loose. The smile started deep within her.

"Weapons, no. Grip, yes. Turn 'em over. I don't feel like bleeding out tonight, young lady. Hit me with the flat sides, if you can actually hit me, that is. Jace, how bout we switch to my playlist?" The beginning themes of Celldweller's "Unshakeable" nearly rattled the room.

"That's a little aggressive for you, Detective, isn't it?"

Ryan smirked in response. He crouched in a Wing Chun stance and beckoned her to come closer. "Bring it, Samurai."

Delight arced through her body. Weapons, play... "I would never hit you with the sharp edge. I have trained too long for that to happen. No need to switch my grip."

She winked. The wakizashi danced in an intricate pattern in her left hand. She sidestepped around him, her feet dancing along the floor, always moving, never resting. With immortal speed, she darted in letting her katana sing as it moved through the air, only to dart out again, dancing.

Ryan smiled. "Nice moves. I think I've seen those before. Where was that? Oh yeah, last time I went to the barber shop. Where's your killer instinct, girl? I thought you were an assassin."

"Nice try." She smiled. "I'm not trying to kill you, talker. I'm trying to get you moving. Thought you wanted to play with me."

"Okay, I'll lead." Ryan offered and launched forward in a series of strikes. His baton clanged loudly off of Shia's blocks as she parried left, right, left, and left again. She ducked under his back kick. His baton struck her katana with a loud ring, inches above her head.

Shia's body lit like fire, delight reaching every cell in her body as she kept Ryan's baton from cracking down on her skull. She twisted, turning into him as she re-sheathed her weapons and slammed her body into his, sending him tumbling back.

To her surprise, Ryan rolled with her throw, dropping his baton and catching his arm above her ribs. They tumbled, together, across the hardwood until momentum stopped them. Shia wound up straddled atop the Detective.

She panted, the smile never leaving her face. She hadn't trained, played, like this since she was still human, or perhaps not, in this other state. She rested her hands on his bare chest, awareness flaring through her at the skin on skin contact.

"Detective, I don't think..." She started.

Ryan reached both hands to her face and pulled her close, his lips meeting hers. She didn't stop him, didn't summon supernatural powers or draw forth hidden blades. Instead, she softened.

He kissed her. It was the only choice. The only path. Shia Ronin stopped fighting him. She stopped being surprised. Her lips met his. Her hands stopped pushing him away. Her tongue touched his and everything else disappeared.

She melted against his touch, finding the harmony between them. She leaned her body against his. Ryan wrapped his arms around her.

An alarm rang in the air. Ryan grabbed at his ears and saw Shia do the same.

"This is an emergency," Jace stated in his electronic voice above the sirens. "Ariel Petrenko has been sighted."

Ariel Petrenko walked slowly, her Doc Marten boots crunching the several inches of snow beneath her feet. She forced her way across Glover Park, searching the tombstones as she walked. Her destination shouldn't be difficult to find. Burying Tyler Daniels in the historic Holy Rood Cemetery required pulling strings. His was the first body buried in the historic graveyard in nearly a century. It was important. The demon had reminded Ariel again and again just how important it was. The ancient ground was the required place for the ritual. She could hear Rachnelle's voice in her head constantly now.

She moved in the shadows, hiding from the floodlights on the side of Holy Trinity Catholic Church. She watched the footsteps she left, hoping to retrace them when the time came to escape. She prayed the police wouldn't track her. She wouldn't have been there at all, but she couldn't keep Rachnelle's tempting voice out of her ear.

"Why does the sun go on shining? Why does the sea rush to shore? Don't they know it's the end of the world, 'cause you don't love me anymore?"

Rachnelle whispered the song into her ear, and Ariel continued searching the graveyard. She stopped, realizing she had almost passed it. She was so caught up in her despair she'd almost missed her destination. She raised her flashlight in a trembling hand, and it revealed the words she had been searching for. She brought her free hand to her mouth. Tears streamed down her face.

"In Memory of Tyler Daniels - Desperate Soul with Unfulfilled Vision. August 1998 - November 2015."

Rachnelle's voice continued to sing, but now the words were her own. "Rise, my angel. There is much to be done. Do not suffer for his deeds or his words. Your life is now your own, and the future is ours to write together."

"I'm not ready for this." Ariel's whisper cracked.

"Of course you are," she whispered in reply. "We need to complete the ritual."

Ariel stared at the carving on the tombstone. She fell to her knees and dropped her flashlight into the snow. "I didn't want him to suffer this."

The voice surrounding her seemed to sigh. "He deserved what he got, my dear."

Ariel buried her face in her hands, sobbing. "Please?"

"Please," Rachnelle replied, "please what?"

The teenager stopped sobbing long enough to gather her thoughts. She wiped her nose on the back of her glove. "Please, let me say good bye."

Rachnelle replied in song, her voice seeming to harmonize with itself. "I thought we'd see forever but forever's gone away. It's so hard to say goodbye to yesterday."

Ariel rose to one knee, pushing her hand against the snow. She lifted her face. The snow fell on her face, which felt warm beneath the tears. She had felt this warm before; once before, under the blanket of shame Tyler Daniels laid on her. She gritted her teeth, staring at the headstone. "It's time. I'm ready."

She followed Rachnelle's whisper in her ear. "Vita nihil aliud somnium. Sed pulchurm est somnium mihi."

Jace translated on the fly, "Life is nothing but a dream. But for me, it's a beautiful dream."

Ryan pulled the steering wheel left, right, and left again. The Impala answered his every command. "What does that mean, Jace?"

"It's part of the ritual," Shia answered before the AI could respond.

Ryan stole a look to the passenger seat. Shia sat in Lotus position, her eyes closed, her breathing slow and steady. A stillness radiated about her entire form. A moment was all he could spare in the crosstown traffic. "What's her endgame? What is she hoping to accomplish?"

Shia exhaled. "Ariel isn't the one with an end game. It's the Lilin who has the resolution in mind."

"How do we stop her?" he asked between gritted teeth.

"I told you before. I've never faced a Lilin."

Ryan ripped the wheel to the side, stomping on the brakes. The Impala slid through the snow, stopping inches away from the fence surrounding the park. "Maybe this is your chance."

Ariel's footsteps were easy to follow. They seemed to burn a path through the snow. Ryan raised his flashlight, but Shia walked before him outside of the range. She focused somewhere he couldn't see, and the drifts of snow didn't slow her down. He shook his head, pulled his pistol from his shoulder holster and followed. They walked a straight line behind the first set of tombstones. They turned a corner, and he stopped.

Steam and smoke rose in the air. Shia stood tall, a silhouette against the rising glow behind her. Ryan rushed to her side. He saw what she was focusing on. The snow melted in an oddly-shaped circle, with gaps in several areas. As if she sensed his curiosity, Shia pointed a finger, at the top of the circle, then the lower right corner. She followed it with the lower right, upper right, and upper left corners. Her fingers seemed to leave a glowing path behind them. The result was a odd shape resembling a pentagram, and the tattoo shared by all the murder victims.

"Is this?"

Shia shook her head. "All dreams must end, Ryan, even the beautiful dreams."

Ryan looked in every direction, half snow-blind. "Where is she?"

Shia lowered her head, breathing and tracing circles in the air. "She's gone. She's finished this part of the ritual."

"This part?"

"Yes."

Ryan scowled. "What's the next part?"

Shia inhaled and exhaled slowly, her breath steaming in the cold air. She turned to face him. "The Lilin must finalize her transition to this world."

He nodded, trying to follow along. "What's the exclamation point on the ritual?"

"A blood sacrifice. She must kill her hostess."

CHAPTER 18

"I don't know what to say, Ryan."

Ryan shook his head, slapping his open palm on the steering wheel in frustration. "Just say yes, CC. I got a bonus at work, and I want the kids to have a good time. Promise me you'll accept it as an early Christmas present and enjoy yourselves and send lots of pictures."

Ryan could picture his sister's smile through the phone. "It's just, I don't know what to say. DJ has been asking for months to go to LEGOLAND, but with the finances so tight, we couldn't make any promises. He's going to be blown away."

"Good, Tell him it's Santa, not me. I don't want him taking it easy on me on the battlefield."

"Okay, but I don't know how to thank you."

Ryan sighed. "I'm working on something pretty bad right now, sis. Promise me you and the fam will get out of town for a long weekend. I'd feel a lot better if you did."

CC paused. "You're spooked, huh?"

"Promise me and don't let Dan get all worked up about it. Tell him to bring a bottle of Noah's Mill to the Super Bowl party, and we're even."

The giggle on the other end of the phone made Ryan picture his sister as a kid. A smile found its way to his lips.

"Okay, big bro, but if I'm going to suddenly ship my family out to Florida, you're going to make me a promise in return."

"Whatever you want, sis."

"Catch the bad guy. Save the day. Be the hero your niece and nephew always talk about. Got it?"

Ryan chuckled. "Yes, ma'am, now go pack your bags. I'm jealous as hell. LEGOLAND sounds kick ass."

CC blew him a kiss over the phone and parted with a "love you, big bro."

Ryan stared at the console of the Impala until his eyes dried out. He'd issued a BOLO, a 'be on the lookout', for Ariel Petrenko, and Jace was pulling out all the stops to find her. House money was on the AI from the future, but it never hurt to have feet on the street doing their jobs, too. Getting his sister and her family out of town might have been sheer paranoia, but the last thing Ryan wanted was for someone he loved to get hurt. The demon hadn't traveled outside DC, so Winter Haven, Florida, was probably pretty safe.

Back to unsafe. Where was Ariel Petrenko going to show her face next? He thought back to what Shia had told him in the graveyard.

Jace answered Ryan's call to Shia, stating she was meditating and doing her own research. Ryan made sure the AI knew to have Shia contact him once she was able. The AI politely responded, and the detective hung up. One fast food chicken sub later, Ryan crossed town and stopped in on the Shaw residence. The surveillance team had reported no trace of Ariel on site, but the Shaw's were a protective and overbearing couple. If Ariel was missing, they'd know where she was, or at least, where she claimed to be. He took the stairs to the Shaw residence two at a time, knocking on the door with a closed fist.

It took three separate sets of knocking before the door opened. Leslie Shaw opened the door slightly, peering at him above the chain that held the door in place. "Oh, Detective, I am so sorry. I was in the basement doing my afternoon yoga." The door closed and then opened, revealing Mrs. Shaw's sweaty tee shirt and tights. "Won't you come in?"

Ryan offered a practiced smile. "Thanks, Mrs. Shaw. If it's okay, I have a few follow up questions."

Leslie Shaw smiled back. "Absolutely, please come in. How can we help you?"

The housewife almost darted down the hall toward the kitchen to prepare a pot of coffee. Ryan eyed the varying family photos that covered the hallway. "Should I kick off my boots here?"

"Don't worry about it. I'll have the housekeeper take care of things when she comes. You take your coffee black, right?"

"Yeah, I mean, yes, thank you," Ryan replied. "Is your daughter here, Mrs. Shaw?"

"Oh, heavens, no," came the reply from the kitchen, "she's at work."

"Work?"

"Yes, she's a clerk at All Things Goth. I told Matthias I thought it was the wrong environment for her, but she really took to it, and he insisted a retail job builds character, especially for a young woman of Ariel's age."

Ryan pulled out his phone and uploaded the information to Jace.

Leslie Shaw emerged in the hallway with a steaming cup of coffee as Ryan finished typing. "Is this about the missing persons' case?"

Ryan took the coffee cup with a nod. "Yes, ma'am, I'm hoping to have this thing all wrapped up, and to be out of your hair as soon as possible. You and your family have been very cooperative. I'm sorry to drag you through all this."

"It's no bother. We love Ariel so much." The woman replied, reaching out to touch a family picture on the wall. "I only hope we haven't put you out, Detective."

"No, ma'am," Ryan replied quickly, "and may I say, you brew a mean cup of java."

Leslie Shaw laughed. "It's nothing. The machine does all the work."

Ryan forced back a laugh. He thought of Jace. Wouldn't we be surprised at what the machines did in the future?

"What about your family, Detective? Are you close?"

Mrs. Shaw's question slapped Ryan in the face like an icy gauntlet. "My family?"

"Of course. Isn't there a Mrs. Detective out there?"

Ryan stuttered and tried to regain his position in the conversation. He didn't get the chance. "Heh, No, ma'am, I'm afraid I haven't had the fortune."

Leslie Shaw smiled. "You haven't asked her yet." She shook her head and offered a knowing smile. "Don't worry. Matthias didn't ask me until he was so seasick no one else would offer him a sympathetic gaze. Poor guy was turning green by the pool. No one told him to take Dramamine before the symptoms started. When the time is right, you'll know."

Ryan took a long pull from his coffee cup. "You said 'All Things Goth', is that right, Mrs. Shaw?"

A knowing look crossed the bottle blonde's eyes. "Yes, Detective. Good luck finding what you're looking for."

Ryan left the Shaw residence feeling like the joke was on him. He immediately called up the only punching bag he could think of. "Jace, employment history for Ariel Petrenko. My bet is there's no way on Earth she's working a mall job Friday and Saturday nights."

The AI responded, "All Things Goth have four outlets within a 30-mile radius of the Shaw household. None of these outlets have an employment record for Ariel Petrenko."

"Does anyone?"

"No, sir."

"Then we need something else. All Things Goth is a vanilla outlet mall shop. That doesn't fit Ariel."

"She does appear to live the Goth lifestyle, Detective."

Ryan closed his eyes and thought. "A typical Goth girl doesn't call up demons, Jace, nor is she targeted as a potential host, right?"

"Statistically..."

"Something extreme happened to Ariel to make the connection." He rubbed his temples, and then lifted his head. "Extreme. A life of extremes. Damn!"

Jace processed as much of Ryan's statements as he could. "Where would you have me search, Detective?"

"Can you map emotions? Are there areas particularly appealing to a Succubus?"

"The female versions of the Incubi are drawn to heightened synapses. They frequently pose as prostitutes or willing participants in S&M. They may also frequent sex shops."

"Damn it," Ryan snapped. "Okay, Jace. I need you to check the following places for me. Don't reply with a question, or I'll have Shia reprogram you as a Mezzosoprano, understood?"

Ryan measured the pause before Jace responded. "Where would you have me search, Detective?"

"You already infiltrated the local banks, credit unions and Metro camera networks, right?"

"Yes."

"Good," Ryan answered, feeling like he had a wild card to play, "I've learned a lot about the pulse of DC. On the job, Jace. Here's where I want you to look..."

CHAPTER 19

Bound was a legend in DC. The founding father of all fetish clubs. It wasn't a location. It was an experience. Bound set the stage for a weekly night of unspoken pleasures. It was the alternate reality shared by the city's adventurous lovers. They could be anyone they wanted. All the order and all of the rules of the uptight, political Nation's Capital disappeared once someone entered the playground. The playground never stayed in one place. It followed the vibe throughout the city. Bound moved from place to place over the years, but the fire and desire of its patrons never wavered.

Ryan hadn't explained how he knew about it. Shia asked and didn't follow up at his silence. He opened the door for her, and they entered. His eyes strayed downward over her petite, tight form before he mentally shook himself. Bass drums pounded with a techno-industrial beat. Bodies flowed between one another on the dance floor. In the corners, leather and latex clad figures watched, or engaged one another, feeling the undeniable passion in the room. This place was about letting inhibitions go. It was about breaking rules and losing titles. The real life version of alternate reality sex games.

Ryan wore a black leather coat over a Steampunk shirt and leather like PVC pants he bought from Rivithead. The leather offered some protection and some camouflage. He placed a protective hand on the small of Shia's bare back on instinct. Too many eyes in the room. Too much energy to power a sex demon. The touch of his hand against her skin seemed to anchor him, to provide him a safe way back from the stormy waters.

"See anything?" he asked, looking around at the festivities.

Shia glanced at him; he could see humor and a hint of something more in her eyes. "I see all sorts of things... Ryan."

She'd almost made a mistake, a gaffe. She wasn't used to working with someone else when hunting, tracking. She glanced around, shifted slightly against his hand, loving the feel of it resting against her skin. It brought a certainty to a very uncertain place. Her dress, if you could call it that, was an interesting mix of black cotton, polyester, zippers and chains. She wasn't too sure about the collar around her neck, but at the same time, she wasn't about to balk at it, since it was keeping the remainder of the dress in place. She was more pleased with the wedge style pleather ankle boots on her feet. Those, those looked like she could kill things with them.

"What are you seeing?" She turned her head, her long hair falling over her back and his hand.

"A whole lot of things a cop isn't supposed to see, much less enjoy." He shifted his gaze from side to side. Looking into her eyes would mean pulling her closer and giving in to the energy, and probably getting the crap kicked out of him. He was already fighting the fire of having his hand on the barc skin of hcr back. Instead, he looked for Ariel. He had been in her room. He had talked music with her. If she was here, she couldn't be hard to find. "What about you? Anything tripping your senses? Anything Jace is chirping at you that will help?"

Jace was, surprisingly, quiet in both their ears. He watched as Shia played with the diamond stud in her right ear, but shook her head. "Quiet."

Her head tilted, her blacker than black hair, tickling his hand as she moved to look around the room. "Lots of sex energy. Perfect for a succubus."

"I'm going to get us a drink," he said, not suggested. His eyes were on the bar at the far end of the room. "I won't be long. Feel like dancing?"

She nodded at him in what he hoped was understanding. She only paused long enough to lean up and brush his cheek with her lips. Maybe she whispered something.

If so, he hadn't heard it. He was damned sure the girl behind the bar was Ariel Petrenko. It was time to ask her the few questions he hadn't during their last visit. Not to mention, the young one wasn't even old enough to be behind the bar.

Shia swayed to the music, feeling the deep bass and pounding guitars of the Sisters of Mercy song all the way down into her bones. Her heart vibrated. She hadn't been in a club like this in centuries. It reminded her of the old Roman orgy parties. This modern day one though, required all men come with a female of their own on their arm. It seemed to be up to the women to pick and choose who they wanted to dance or play with. Several of the single women wound their way through the mass of bodies. Rule was, if a man wanted into the club, he had to be on the arm of a woman, yet the women held no such rule in reverse. She wondered when the rules had changed. Not that she'd paid attention to any of it in a long time. The old Roman orgies used to be frequented by the sisters if only to keep the demon calling in check. Although, Raisa had offered to keep a check over the years. Too many times the sex rites had unwittingly unleashed hell on earth for more than a few days at a time. She'd have to check in with the Russian about them.

Her glance strayed to the gauzy curtained seating area. Her keen eyesight made out exactly what was going on behind those curtains, not that they were fooling anyone. Hands strayed over bodies, lips locked on lips, or moving even lower, and some of the men merely watched the women with each other. Others reached out to participate here or there, a hand grazing an almost bare nipple, caressing a hip, and sometimes more. Her pulse quickened. You couldn't walk into one of these places without the energy affecting you. She'd learned in her early years she was no different than others in this instance, feeling the heightened sex energy. She refrained from letting it pull her in, instead hovering on the fringes.

Ryan worked his way past the mingling bodies, not even looking at the small station where a dominatrix was teaching the art of hanging by fishhooks. He concentrated on the girl behind the bar. From across the room, he would have sworn, under oath, she was Ariel. As he grew closer, he grew less confident, less sure of himself, and less comfortable with all of it.

He started to sweat.

His skull pounded in beat with the bass pumping around them. Ryan gritted his teeth and tried to breathe through the dizziness. Too many people in the club. Not enough air. Maybe.

He shook it off and continued to approach, one step at a time. He heard the music change behind him, something distant, an echo. Right now, the entire club was an echo. He was delayed. He looked up again at the girl behind the bar and nearly vomited.

He squeezed his eyes shut.

The dizziness buzzed in his head like a swarm of hornets. He leaned on the wall. Reaching into his sports jacket, he pulled out his sunglasses. There were plenty of other men in here tonight wearing them. Maybe they were trying to hide their eyes from the women they were observing. Ryan chuckled in his head. He wasn't so different.

He concentrated on the floor, head up, eyes down. He reached the bar without losing swagger or momentum. He sat on a stool and raised a finger, watching the bar top instead of the girl behind it. Staring at her made his head swim, but he could look down and recognize her shadow when she came close. "Can I get a drink here, please?"

Shia didn't move away when a warm body moved closer to hers. The other body hesitated in drawing too close until she flashed a look. A brunette, slim, maybe in her early thirties, tastefully dressed even with a few chains and hooks in her outfit swayed into her. She had a red and black blindfold painted on her face, complete with embedded rhinestones. She moved a hand over Shia's gloved arms, her red nails sparkling in the lights. She looked at Shia with bedroom eyes and a slow smile.

She categorized the woman in a blink of an eye. Not desperate, her smile genuine despite the outfit. Shia smiled back, moving a little closer, dancing with her.

She'd blend in, if only to hunt her prey. Sex energy was so hard to work around or even with. The woman leaned closer, as close as Ryan had to Shia earlier. She wrapped her arms around Shia's shoulders as she dipped her hips, clearly expressing her willingness to be led in the dance. Then she rose again, swaying to the music.

Shia let the other woman dance closer intrigued for a brief moment, missing the art of dance, but her eyes still wandered back over the crowd of people, looking for Ryan realizing as much fun as the brunette could be, she'd rather be dancing with her detective.

She stopped for a brief moment, so brief, only Ilsa would have noticed.

She'd rather be dancing with Ryan? She didn't dance. She didn't want. Yet, she distinctly wanted his hands on her rather than the brunette's.

She stepped back in a sultry swing, still smiling at her partner yet dancing away.

She sensed the Lilin's presence, but here and there, detected the presence of a few other otherworldly beings. A few vamps hovered on the fringes of the dance floor, hesitating as if they could sense her energy nearby. She didn't want to startle them into causing a ruckus when she was on the trail of one dealing in death. So long as they refrained from killing the humans, she let them walk in peace. She only drew her sword when required to restore the balance.

Ryan had retreated to the bar, getting them drinks, scoping out the place. It wasn't a big place, but rather narrow, and they had several floors to search. Apparently, each floor had a theme. Based on this one, she couldn't wait to see what the other ones held in store. She turned to look for him. He wasn't at the side bar. She couldn't find him among the patrons on the dance floor.

Finally, she spotted him sitting at the back bar and frowned. He had a rather odd look on his handsome face and was wearing sunglasses. She glanced over his shoulder at the bartender who had a panicked look on hers.

What the...?

An orange aura flared to life around the bartender and ripped across the club, flowing into a woman several hundred feet away from her and closer to the exit. Shia started. She had seen that aura before. The Succubus and Incubus had a very specific color in the spectrum of spiritual energy.

The demon had detected her hunters and was making a move.

Shia's jaw tightened. This succubus was not going to kill another human host and whatever male she lured into her trap. One more killing and all her closed cases would be reopened, and the news awash with the idea of a serial killer on the loose in the streets of DC. She didn't want to clean that mess up.

"Thanks for the dance, beautiful." She tossed over her shoulder before weaving her way through the club. The woman smiled and winked her before blending back into the crowd of other dancers.

She couldn't use her preternatural speed in here without causing injury. While she wasn't planning on returning to this establishment, she also wasn't looking to leave it in a shambles for the patrons who'd sought out love in various manners. She weaved around bodies pressed to bodies, never letting the tall blond ahead of her out of her sight. She didn't lash out when people stumbled into her, instead ducking and sidestepping the best she was able.

The woman leaned up and kissed the bouncer on the cheek as she stepped past him. Shia caught the glance and the smile the succubus tossed her way. The demon had the audacity to wiggle her rhinestone-encrusted fingers in a wave as she continued on outside.

"She's on foot, m'lady. She won't get too far ahead of you." Jace stated in her ear now she could hear him as she neared the door. He'd been quiet in the club, thankfully. She didn't need him blowing an eardrum to be heard over the blare of the music.

The bouncer, a big guy with a military haircut, sporting the usual tight black shirt and cargo pants, stepped in her way. It never failed, this preference for basic black. At least this club was a little more subtle, he didn't have 'security' sprawled across his chest or back.

"Where do you think you're going?" His arms crossed over his chest. She smiled. Big guy, lots of gym time she'd bet. He'd lose in an all-out fight in 10-seconds.

"Out. I need air." She said, fanning herself with her hand, not that she had much on to begin with. Ankle boots and short black dress did wonders for her ego when Ryan's eyes lit on her, but left nothing to hide, no weapons but her body.

"Not without your date, you're not." He answered.

Shia didn't hesitate, instead struck, a rapid combination to his solar plexus, ribs and throat, and left him bent over gasping for air, tears streaming down his face.

"Next time,...oh, forget it, there won't be a next time. My date will be right behind me." She pushed the door open, stepping into the cold night air. Her eyes adapted to the lighting, and the trail flared brilliantly to her right.

"Keep track of me so Ryan can follow." She told Jace.

"He's not far behind you." The AI answered. "She miscalculated and turned down a dead end behind the club."

"Gotta love those dead ends." At least she wasn't going to have to run after her in high heels, and she'd had the sense, fashion sense to wear some killer boots. Although, she was certain the woman the succubus had jumped into was wearing stilettos. She'd need to avoid those sharp points.

She turned the corner behind the club, ducking seconds before the knife hand struck. She rolled into the snow, anticipating the first strike. She shifted immediately, avoiding the high heel thrown at her head.

"Seriously?" She sighed as she rolled up to standing with the spiked heel in hand, thankful for the boots she'd selected to go with her outfit. Fighting in the snow, in bare feet, sucked. She played with the heel, looking at it, pretending to study it. "You're a demon, and you threw a shoe at my head?"

Rachnelle answered, her voice unnatural through the painted lips of the tall blonde woman in the tight, black latex. "They were beginning to bite into my ankles. Such a nuisance, like a samurai with visions of immortality. You don't appeal to my palette, young one. Go away and let me do what I was called to do."

"Oh, I get that the heels bite, fashion sucks. But, I promise, I don't have visions of immortality. I've asked to die a thousand times over. But you, your kind, keep calling me back, because you won't behave. You can't handle me and my sisters."

"Certainly you're older than these sheep you protect, but you don't know forever. Don't confuse your life with forever. You're meant to stand longer than those around you. You're a Sequoia. The sheep can drive through your hollowed out body while you age on for centuries, but in the end, you'll wind up as ash and smoke. Lay down and die, little one."

"Forever?" Shia tilted her head, rising to her full

height, strong stance, as strong as her damn dress and boots would allow. "Forever is nothing. It is a drop in the bucket. If I end up as ash and smoke, so be it. I did my job, I served my calling. I've died. I have never laid down to do so, but I have died, over and over again. And you know what, Baita, I will continue to do so. Because it is what I am called to do, that is who I am."

Rachnelle sneered, and her face betrayed any human emotion. Her teeth curled into fangs. Her eyes pooled blood. The skin pulled against her bones, looking skeletal and gaunt. She hissed, a sound no human could make. And then she launched.

Three steps closed the distance between them as the Lilin slammed into Shia, taking her off of her feet and driving her into the cold, wet snow. Her claws dug into Shia's shoulders. She rocked her head from side to side, a proud display of the horns she would bare in her true form.

Shia focused as she rolled in the snow with the demon. This, this is what she lived for.

Bring it.

When the succubus slammed into her body, she rolled, taking them both over and up, pushing with all her might and tossing the woman away from her.

"Really? Omae o korosu." She said as the blonde landed in the snow a few feet away from her. She needed to kill the demon.

She couldn't kill the human host. Well, she could, but her Code wouldn't allow it. She needed the demon out of the human body so she could kill it. It couldn't be allowed to remain in a living host.

The blonde girl in the black dress crossed her arms and began shivering. Her blood red eyes shifted to distant, confused, azure blue. Her lips quivered and actually began changing colors. She looked up at the falling snow. Confusion fell over her face. "Why are we out here?"

Shia stopped, a moment, and then, tilted her head listening, sensing, and watching the energy patterns. "Yeah, no dice, baita. Try again. I've dealt with your kind before. The innocent always dies. I know this."

The blonde nodded in agreement as arms thick as legs wrapped around Shia, forcing the breath from her lungs. She tried to gain her footing in the snow, but she was lifted from the ground. She briefly recognized the scent of the security guard behind her. The echo of Rachnelle's inhuman laughter rang in her ears.

"Shia!" She heard her name.

She heard his shout, Ryan's call.

The massive arms of the bouncer tightened around her.

Ryan unsheathed her katana, which he had worn between his shirt and blazer all night. He slid it forward, and it burned through the snow like a flare. Then he launched into the air, slamming his elbows down on both collarbones of the bouncer. The man's left hand released immediately. His right hand released a second later. Ryan reloaded and drove another strike into the big man's neck. The bouncer fell with a grunt into the snow.

Shia pushed them apart, rolling forward. The hilt of her katana rested in the snow between her feet. She reached for it, snagging it without effort, rolling in the snow with her sword arcing up and slicing, a clean hit, through the woman's leg. The only safe hit she could make, the only honorable one.

The blonde went down on one knee, an unholy cry issuing from her lips. Shia watched as the orange aura retreated.

She leaned back in the snow, panting. That demon was one hell of a fighter.

Ryan watched the orange glow dissipate over his head. He ran to Shia, supporting her. "Talk to me."

"I'm fine. Go." She said, as her head lolled back. She needed to reset, recuperate.

The blonde lay in the snow next to them, hurt, but not a life threatening injury. All hints lead back to the original host, the trail leading out of the one laying in the snow.

"She's going back to Ariel. Go. I can take care of this." She said. She pushed him and pushed her sword back to him as well.

Ryan stared into her eyes, finding strength and devotion as he did so. "Yeah, not so much." He reached for his radio. "Dispatch, I need a bus. We have a female victim, mid-30's, possible target of a date rape attack. We also have a 20-something male with multiple blunt force wounds to the neck, skull and abdomen, probably a ganger gone rogue on the whole Raver scene. Get us one as soon as you can. I'll try to contain the scene, but you know the routine."

Ryan leaned down to Shia. "Bound is a fetish club. There's no surveillance footage. Those cameras are empty. You need to be somewhere else, and I can't leave these two alone with broken bones and lacerations. Let's get you somewhere safe. I have a voice in my ear willing to be my valet. That okay with you?"

Shia looked up, her arms looped around his neck, and said, "Ok, just get me to your car, and then follow."

CHAPTER 20

"We are in position, Detective." Patrick O'Shaughnessy's Irish voice boomed over the intercom.

Ryan nodded to himself. "I only hope you have the full dozen donuts, O'Sho," he replied.

The veteran officer laughed in response. "A dozen each, you gym rat. We'll let you know if your Goth girl shows up on our watch."

"Roger that," Ryan replied between shortened breaths to restore his composure. The other stations confirmed the same. Uniformed officers awaited Ariel Petrenko at Bound, her foster home, the Greenleaf Medical Center, and her last two places of employment, Madam Reynards' House of Nails and Little Empire's Late Night Pizza.

Ryan pulled the Impala through the snow to the curb opposite the cemetery. He killed the engine, and the steady roar of the Impala went quiet. Silence owned the moment. Snow fell and melted on the windshield. The faint glow of the heads-up display reflected on his face. He made out Shia's reflection in the passenger seat. She hadn't said a word. He stole a longer glance. Her eyes were closed, her breathing steady.

He closed his eyes, his thoughts going to his family. Flings peppered his history. He had a high school girlfriend for almost two years, but he had never really loved a woman other than his mother, his sister, and his niece. CC agreeing to get out of town brought a peace he couldn't explain. Right now, he wanted the same solace as he thought of Shia. She was battle-tested and knew more pain than he could ever feel, but all he wanted to do was to get her somewhere safe.

Ryan looked back at her. In the blue glow of the Impala's LED, she looked tired. Maybe it was his imagination, but for the first time, he could see her history. He could see the centuries she had seen as a shield for others. She was unlike any being he could remember. He reached a hand out to brush the hair from her face.

"I am all right, if you are concerned," Shia said as his hand brushed her cheek.

Ryan stopped but did not pull his hand away. "I'm not sure that's the right word."

Her eyes remained closed, but she didn't tense up or object. She simply exhaled. "What is the proper word?"

He smiled, completely out of his comfort zone. "I don't know. I guess...Fascinated, maybe?"

She turned to face him, and when she opened her eyes, her presence filled every cell of his body. His reaction must have been evident because she paused. She stared at him out of pure curiosity. "What do you see?"

Ryan's breath caught in his chest. He tried to speak once, then again. Finally, the words found his lips. "I see you."

Shia closed her eyes once more and took in a deep breath. When she exhaled, she closed the distance between them. Her lips met his, and the world disappeared. She was pure energy in his arms. She was warmth. She was desire. She was worlds he couldn't comprehend.

She was home.

They had a moment in bliss, but only a moment. Ryan's phone rang. They held onto each other for another breath, wishing away the rest of the world. Shia finally pulled away. She nodded briefly, mouthing the word's "it's okay."

Ryan tapped on the button to answer the call. Patrick O'Shaughnessy's voice filled the interior of the car. "You got your ears on, lead foot?"

Ryan cursed, but hope danced at the edges of his vision. O'Sho and his team were watching Tyler Daniel's grave. He tapped the phone and bolted upright. "What have you got?"

"I've got an empty dozen donuts and a confirmed sighting of your Goth girl. She's here, like you said she'd be."

Ryan's tone alone sent Shia into motion. "Hold your position. We're on our way."

Ariel shuddered against the snowfall. She hadn't worn enough layers. She shook her head. No number of layers would warm the cold she felt. The snow crept in between her Doc Marten boots and her cargo pants. The cold seeped into anywhere it could find. She shivered, trying to find the way to his gravesite. Finally, she found it through blind luck, snow blind luck. She read the words on the headstone. Tears swelled in her eyes, even as she struggled to re-kindle the flame he had once lit within her.

Ariel had been adopted and returned into the Foster care system several times. She was the consolation prize for families who didn't get their first choice. Her adoptive family had turned her away, not once, but twice, before she was supposed to be placed with the Shaws. She was doubtful. She was scared.

And then, along came Tyler Daniels.

He was bold, brash, and confident. He wasn't the typical orphan. He knew how to play guitar, and he was going to be the rags-to-riches success story America loved so much. When he first approached her at Greenleaf, Ariel had frozen. His sly smile stopped her in his tracks. The next few weeks, they exchanged glances, smiles. Then came his first online message.

"Ariel, I love the way the sun glows on your skin. Don't you dare change seats during lunch or you'll break my heart. I look forward to seeing more of you, Tyler."

Their relationship continued, under the radar, for two more months. He complimented her, and she replied. Finally, one day, he offered something more. She shivered, remembering his message.

She shook as she stared down at Tyler's headstone. "You lied to me." She wrapped her arms around her body. "You promised me we would be together, and we would have a family. You used me. I let you do things. I let you use me, and then you punished me."

Tears filled Ariel's eyes. "You forced yourself on me, and when I accepted you, you laughed. You laughed."

She sobbed openly.

Shia stopped and listened. She caught the words of the young woman in the twisting breeze. "You don't love me, you don't love me," Ariel continued in a whirlwind of emotions. "You can't see how I matter in this world, even though I loved you. You couldn't see me for who I am." She sensed the dark energy respond. She clenched her hands on the handles of her swords.

"O'Sho, drop back," Ryan said into the radio. "This is about to get violent."

Shia studied the girl for several moments. A small, feminine voice seemed to carry from the figure, sobs echoing in the winter air. Her shoulders bobbed several times and twice she raised an arm to wipe her nose on a sleeve. The orange aura clung to her like an unwanted parasite. The girl sniffed, wrapping her arms around her body, chilled inside and out. Shia could make out a few words as she approached. "Please, I don't want this. I never wanted this."

"Ariel," Shia slid her katana from its scabbard, letting the tip rest in the snow. Her words came out with puffs in the cold air surrounding them. When this was all over, she was putting in time for a warm weather jaunt. "Succubi are never out for anyone or anything other than themselves. It is their very nature to hunt and kill. She's not going to bring a man to you. She's going to keep using you so she can hunt until your spirit is drained from carrying her too long. Then she'll find a new host. She has used you to kill. She killed Tyler."

She knew the demon whispered in Ariel's ear. She could see the orange aura intensifying as the succubus attempted to pull the girl more into her energetic pattern.

"You need to send her back. What was the spell you used to call her?" Shia asked. "It's not too late to send her back."

Ariel turned around. Tears streaked down her face. She clutched a bent and folded piece of paper against her chest. She sobbed. "No! She is all I have left. She can save me."

Shia spoke the words Jace whispered in her ear. She recognized the words of their original tongue, a language that proceeded human communications. The glowing silhouette of the Beast exited Ariel's body, fighting against the edges of its cage. Fiery eyes glanced at the samurai as it tested the boundaries of its containment. Shia evaluated the situation. She could keep Rachnelle contained, but the Lilin would devour her innocent host in the interim. Her only other choice was to destroy the circle of containment and to face the daughter of Lilith face to face.

Shia stood to her full height, her katana cut through the night, slicing through the circle that now glimmered faintly on the ground. An unholy shriek ripped from Ariel's mouth as the orange energy of the succubus, Rachnelle, spiraled out of her.

"Bring it on, demon," she dared.

Rachnelle hissed as Shia's blade cut through the power circle. She had lost her hostess. She had lost containment, and now, she was mere energy in the air. The Lilin focused and her energy became tangible. Ariel Petrenko's body fell lifeless into the snow behind her. A noise came from her mouth that was a combination of a hiss and a roar. Her outline twisted and shifted, sometimes feminine, sometimes serpentine.

"You will die for your interference, Samurai," the demon challenged.

The demon's energy shifted the air currents causing the snow around them all to kick up in a mini snownado. Caught up in the small whirling Vortex, Ryan's body lifted and slammed against a marble headstone. He winced, all the air left his body in strong whoosh. When he landed hard against the ground, his hand clutched his ribs, certain they had broken the moment the Lilin released the energy. He forced himself up on one arm lifting from the snow and tried to find Shia.

"You have interrupted my Ritual. My ritual!"

Rachnelle hissed, her dark wings flared out behind her, melting paths in the snow as they swept upwards and back spanning well over eight feet across. Heat radiated from her form in waves, and the snow retreated in her wake.

Shia should have known the demon female would have wings. The melting snow, not so much a show from a demon. She bit back a sigh hoping Jace continued to record everything to be logged later.

"You never should have tried infiltrating this world," Shia responded, raising her blades. "Go home to your unwanted Mother, and the rest of your unwanted kin. You have no place here."

The demon dove, her claws and wings striking with blazing speed. Shia refrained from crying out as one of the poisoned tips scratched along her cheek. Cut her, would she? Her lips flattened, and she countered with her katana and wakizashi, finally landing a single strike on the Lilin's left wing.

Rachnelle roared and drew back. Black blood dripped down over the dark gray of the wing. The tip now hung at an odd angle.

Shia took a deep breath in. "The ritual is ended, demon. Your time here is finished. Go. Home."

"I will have my place on Earth," Rachnelle screeched, rushing forward. She tried to strike again with claws, wings and even snapped her teeth. Shia's blades twisted in circles. Her katana deflected Rachnelle's claw. She parried a follow-up strike with the shorter blade. She twisted her hips to avoid another strike before finding her balance and steadying into a defensive stance. She couldn't afford another cut, even as shallow as the last. Her body worked to counter the poison as it tried to snake its way through her system. She launched a small knife from a hidden palm in her glove. The blade struck the demon's midsection, and she used the pause to rush backward, creating distance.

Rachnelle hissed and rushed forward. Marble tombstones shattered under the energy of her wings. Snow blew everywhere, forced upward by the wind she created. Shia dove, rolling to her feet and driving her swords in a killing blow aimed at the demon.

The katana in her right hand landed in the demon's chest. Shia felt the thrill of victory for only a moment.

Rachnelle seemed to take the killing blow in stride. She batted away the shorter sword, laughing loudly.

The Lilin leveled eyes with the Samurai. The first evidence of vulnerability streaked across her skin. She found her footing, and she smiled at the dynamic of the battlefield.

"You have dealt the killing blow, but I will avenge myself. You've failed, Samurai. And now you and I will become one."

Orange smoke swirled about them both, dancing, cavorting as black smoke weaved in. Shia coughed as the smoke hit her lungs. She held her breath, trying to fight the invasion of the demon. Her chest burned with the need to breathe. Her fingers clamored wildly in search or her second blade. The fringes of vision began to blur. She clenched her teeth. Drawing in breath would mean drawing in the Lilin. Rachnelle would claim her soul as one more victim. She couldn't allow that to happen.

A symphony of voices filled Shia's being. Her master. Ilsa. The four year old she could never name. Her sisters. The many lives she had portrayed and those who depended on her.

Ryan.

She fumbled even as the world grew darker. Figures became shadows. It was all a shadow. Was this it? Was this the end?

Her fingers found the blade of the knife. Shia screamed with every ounce of energy she had. She drove the knife blade upward, slashing Rachnelle's throat. The demon's head rolled. Black and orange smoke flowed forth. Yet the creature's form didn't disintegrate, as it should.

Shia held on. She closed her eyes, two hands now wrapped around the hilt of the katana. It wasn't the way she'd thought she'd go out, her true death, but she'd be damned if she'd let the succubus win and take others with her.

No. More. Others.

The ground trembled beneath her. The winds continued to rip around her. Her hair unknotted and whipped in the air as well. She coughed, the smoke flooding her lungs.

"M'lady." Jace's voice chirped in her ear, and if she could put a feeling to it, the AI sounded frantic.

She coughed, trying to response, but had no air left to do so. She struggled to keep her eyes open, eyes on the Lilin. The ash and dust created a shield. Yet, she refused to release her sword unsure of whether Rachnelle was truly dead. The fire burned in her lungs, and Shia finally drew in a breath. The oxygen rushed into her body, inviting the idea of peace.

Instead of peace, there was Hellfire.

CHAPTER 21

Rachnelle's body began to decompose, orange smoke and black ash replacing her fiery skin. The smoke and ash began to swirl around Shia, who stood motionless. She craned her neck back and opened her mouth in a soundless scream. The smoke and ash encircled her and then poured into her mouth. Her dark eyes changed to orange.

Ryan screamed her name, but if she heard him, she made no signal. He raced to her, calling out to her the entire time. Jace also tried to get her to respond, but she stood, her katana in one hand, her body shaking though she was burning. Ryan finally pushed through the waves of heat coming off of her body and reached her. He grabbed her arm.

Shia was burning.

Fire crept into every ounce of her body. The air in her lungs was pure flame, and her skin boiled. Rachnelle called to her. Her voice was a whisper rising into a thunderclap and then back to near silence. Shia felt all of it. The years of desire. The centuries of rage. She felt the pain of every woman the demon had possessed and sucked dry. She felt that deadly siphoning of her own energy. She fought Rachnelle with her willpower, but the demon was clawing at her spirit from every angle. Shia could keep her at bay, suffering the heat of Hell itself all the while, but for how long? She focused, strengthening her defenses.

And then the sensation of skin on skin. Ryan's touch. It was a fraction of a second, but it was enough for Rachnelle to pierce her defenses.

Rachnelle leveled her gaze at Ryan, orange eyes glowing. She licked her lips, leaning closer. Then, she drove her palm into his chest. Ryan lost his grip on her and tumbled end over end in the melting snow. He rolled gingerly to one knee as she stepped toward him. "Your precious samurai is gone, dog. I will drink every ounce of her until she is nothing more than a withered shell of a being. Will you still lust for her then, dog?"

Ryan rose to his feet. He had lost his gun when she struck him. It was somewhere on the ground along with Shia's shorter sword. The demon wielded Shia's katana. "Oh, no, sister," he replied, "I know she's in there. You're not staying for long. Better find a way back into the ground." He grabbed the baton from his belt, snapping it to full length.

Rachnelle screamed her hissing roar again, and Ryan took a step backward. He was unable to deal with the sound coming out of Shia's body. He gritted his teeth and struck at her. She parried his strike, turning to cut him across the midsection. He evaded and swung a counterstrike that narrowly missed. She swung the katana downward, and he blocked. Before he could strike, she drove an elbow into his already broken ribs.

He doubled over. She brought up her knee and caught him in the nose.

Ryan fell backward, seeing stars. He tasted blood in seconds. He spat the blood out. The taste was familiar. Broken noses were practically a Calder family tradition. The aching in his side and the pain of breathing was a bigger concern.

"Filthy man-beast," Rachnelle addressed him with rage, "fall to your knees and cower before me, and I will make your death quick...after I devour your lover."

Rising to full height, Ryan shook his head. Blood spatter dripped over the snow. He lowered into a Wing Chun fighting stance. "No chance, you old hag. You fight like a girl."

She hissed at him in defiance and launched into a series of strikes. He blocked the first few with the baton. She caught him once, then twice with flesh wounds. He grimaced at the pain the katana delivered, but it was all part of a plan.

Shia's attacks were graceful, coordinated, and fit a pattern. These weren't Shia's attacks. They were vengeful and wild, and traditional defensive moves were only going to hold her at bay before one wild strike found home. Rachnelle struck faster and faster. Ryan parried or evaded, but his breathing was becoming labored, and the taste of blood made his stomach turn.

"I can taste her agony, mongrel. Her suffering is delicious. You will join her soon. Stop this senseless defense and die like the filth you are."

The demon had a point. Quitting would have been easy, but quitting meant Shia would be gone forever. He couldn't let that happen. If there was anything worth fighting for, it was love. If there was anyone worth fighting for, it was Shia.

Ryan had no clever retort, only pain and anger. He struck, catching her arm hard. She lost her defense for a minute, and he brought the baton down with a vengeance. He heard her collarbone snap. Then he stomp-kicked her in the chest with as much force as he could muster.

She should have been on her back ten feet away, but Rachnelle hardly moved. She brought the katana around low, and he parried.

The thousand-year-old sword sliced the baton in two.

The blade continued, slicing into Ryan's left leg above the knee.

He screamed in agony and dropped to the ground. All he felt was the stabbing pain. He grabbed his leg. His hands shake, and his vision blurred by tears.

Rachnelle stood, licking his blood off of the katana blade. She smiled a wide, evil smile.

Ryan knew she was still there, but he could hardly make out her shape. He dug his hands into the ground and pulled himself away from her. He prayed for time, for the impossible.

The demon laughed, and it filled him with a dread horror nearly making him unable to move. Instead, he panicked, and began clawing away from her frantically. His hands struck marble, and he pulled himself up against one of the grave markers. If he could get to his feet, maybe the adrenaline would save his life.

He tugged on the grave marker, making his way halfway up to standing. Rachnelle grabbed his shoulder, and he let out a terrified sound. She pushed him down, turning his shoulders with a flick of her wrist. He landed flat, his back against the grave marker, and his legs splayed out before him on the ground. The demon stood over him, smiling in delight, feeding off of his terror.

"Yes, little dog, shiver. Let me treasure your pain. Your suffering makes the Mother happy. You, all of you human males, must be made to suffer. It is Mother's wish."

She moved lower, straddling him. He cried out in pain again. The pressure on his wounded leg made his vision go white. He could feel himself passing out, and part of him wanted nothing more than that.

"I told you that I would take your life, mongrel." She shifted her weight slightly, and the pain grew even more.

Ryan couldn't look at her. He couldn't stare into those bestial eyes. This was Shia. She was still in there somewhere. She had to be. He was fighting for her. Was she still fighting for him? He whipped his hands around in the snow, looking for something, anything to buy him time.

The blade of Shia's smaller sword cut into the fingers of his left hand as he brushed it. That was it. The blade. Shia's own weapon. Would that break the spell? Would she gain power from her weapon enough to drive out the demon?

Rachnelle brushed a clawed finger down the side of Ryan's face. A trail of blood followed her touch. She leaned close and licked it from his skin. Ryan coughed blood. "Go to Hell, bitch," he said as he spat the blood in her face.

She leaned back just enough. Ryan reached out with his right hand and grabbed a rock the size of a baseball. He brought the rock up to smash the demon in the head, and she blocked the strike easily. She screamed at him, "Filthy mortal."

Ryan's left hand closed around the short sword. He stared into the demon's eyes. "Shia, I love you."

Then he drove the blade upward, piercing her heart.

Orange and black flickers of light rose from Shia's body. There was no sound, no wailing in agony, or pain or vengeance. The flickers of light simply left her body and floated in the air. Slowly, they shifted, coming together, not into a being but into some pattern Ryan couldn't understand. Then, they moved slowly downward, like ash falling to the ground. They gathered on the page that Ariel had held in her hands. The words glowed orange for a few seconds, and then everything was silent.

Shia's lifeless body fell sideways. Ryan leaned over to her. He brushed the hair from her face. He lifted her up to him as best he could. The weight of it all hit him, and he collapsed, sobbing against her, crying her name.

CHAPTER 22

Ryan was dying, but in a way, he was already dead. He was losing blood, and without help, he would join the dead here in the cemetery. It didn't matter. Nothing mattered, not without Shia.

He cradled her body close to his. At least there was some small solace in that fact. They would die together. He silently wished Heaven existed and somehow a thousand-year-old Samurai and a less-than-honorable cop would somehow find each other again. He leaned his forehead against her. Beaten and broken, he couldn't smell her. He tasted only blood, and his eyes began to swell shut. But he could feel her, feel the warmth of her, and it somehow calmed him.

He closed his eyes and prepared to die.

A breath caressed his cheek for a moment and then disappeared. He imagined it. He must have. The breath repeated, and this time, it was accompanied by a whisper. "Ryan."

His left eye opened slightly, and he saw her. Shia was pale, and her eyes seemed darker than he remembered, but she was alive. Her fingers brushed his cheek and, as she did, a peace flowed into him. He felt as if he was outside of his body. There was no pain, no sensation, no sorrow.

"You saved me, warrior. I am alive." Her words seemed like an echo without the original sound.

He felt her touch his face again, and he closed his eyes. Exhaustion overtook him.

"It is your turn to rest. Sleep, Ryan, I am here for you. I will always be here for you."

Flashlights and flares lit the cemetery. The withered trees and grave markers cast long, eerie shadows. Sergeant Patrick O'Shaughnessy shouted frantically at the other uniformed officers searching the area. This was where Ryan had said it would happen. He had told them to hold back. After ten minutes of radio silence, Patrick decided the Detective would need some backup.

There was blood, and an odd patch where the snow had been melted away. The earth was scorched in nearly a perfect circle, but that was it. There was no Ariel. There was no assailant. There was no Ryan.

A younger officer approached the Sergeant. "Still no sign, sir. We're bringing in the K-9 unit now, but we haven't found anything so far."

"Widen the search, then," O'Shaughnessy replied gruffly. "We've got a man missing, dammit. We've got a good man missing."

"Yes, sir," the officer replied and began echoing the instructions into his radio.

The sergeant crouched down to once again inspect the blood-spattered grave marker.

"In Memory of Tyler Daniels - Desperate Soul with Unfulfilled Vision. August 1998 - November 2015."

CHAPTER 23

"You were dead." Ryan managed to say as the medication began to wear off.

Shia sat in lotus position, facing the medical bed on which he rested. "It's not that simple."

"You were dead, Shia. Jesus, you scared the hell out of me."

She rose to her feet and walked to his side. She eyed the screen, double-checking the meds and constant wave of radiology images Jace was providing. She lifted his left hand up and brushed the tips of his fingers with her lips. The scars from her sword blade were already healed over. "And you, apparently, cut Hell out of me."

He half-laughed, half-coughed in reply. "What were you thinking?"

"I told you," she said, placing his hand back down on the bed. "I've never faced a Lilin in battle. I underestimated her. We would both be dead without your efforts."

"My efforts," he tried to sit up but second-guessed the idea when his ribs protested, "Shia, I stabbed you through the heart. I killed you."

"Stop. Please, stop." She sighed, her eyes trailing over his wounds. "You saved me." She looked past him to an area he couldn't see. "And, you saved her."

Ryan turned his head. In an adjacent room, Ariel Petrenko rested, surrounded by monitors and machines.

"How?"

Shia smiled. "We cannot foresee when the Universe will deliver a new sister to us. We only know we are her guides, her protectors. We are her family. And you, Ryan Jonathan Calder, accomplished something no human male throughout history has ever done." She leaned down and kissed him softly. "You delivered a sister to her rightful family."

He smiled back. "I don't know what to say. You're welcome?"

Shia kissed him once more, than pulled back and winked.

"When you're healthy, I will show you just how grateful I am."

"Let us bow our heads in prayer."

Father Francisco Munoz closed his eyes, reciting the Word as he had hundreds of times before. "Soon afterward, He journeyed to a city called Nain, and His disciples and a large crowd accompanied Him. As He drew near to the gate of the city, a man who had died was being carried out, the only son of his mother, and she was a widow. A large crowd from the city was with her. When the Lord saw her, He was moved with pity for her and said to her, 'Do not weep.'"

The priest continued. "He stepped forward and touched the coffin; at this the bearers halted, and He said, 'Young man, I tell you, arise!'"

"The dead man sat up and began to speak, and Jesus

gave him to his mother. Fear seized them all, and they glorified God, exclaiming, 'a great prophet has arisen in our midst, ' and, 'God has visited His people.'"

Father Munoz opened his eyes slowly. "And the people said 'Amen.'"

The voices in attendance Ryan, Shia, Matthias and Leslie Shaw replied in unison. Father Munoz continued, "At this time, we commit Ariel's body to the Earth. In the sweat of thy face shalt thou eat bread, till thou return unto the ground; for out of it wast thou taken: for dust unto art, and unto dust shalt thou return."

Ariel's body, held within a black, oaken coffin was lowered into the ground. The caretakers released the ropes as Father Munoz began.

"Our Father, who art in heaven, hallowed be thy name. Thy kingdom come, as thy will be done, in earth as in Heaven..."

Dr. Shia Ronin snapped at Jace a few more times, and he countered her line of questioning before it began. Eventually, she rolled her eyes, delayed their one-on-one inquisition period and dropped into the passenger seat of the Impala idling beneath her. She immediately switched focus and eyed Ryan. He was adjusting the mirrors to accommodate his point-of-view in the driver's seat. "Fasten your seatbelt, Dr. Ronin, otherwise this futuristic four-wheel vehicle gives me a rash of shit for failing to secure anyone else in the front seat."

She bit her tongue, a thousand responses on the tip of it.

"I agree," Ryan eyed her with a knowing smile. "He probably needs a firmware upgrade to understand what is and isn't legit. Can you make that happen?" He winked, knowing he had put Jace on the defensive.

Shia smiled and laughed.

"Lady Ronin, I can..."

"Shut up, Jace," she replied, staring at Ryan. She shifted her line of questioning from the AI to the detective. "Where are we going, exactly?"

Ryan smiled, his grin making him seem like a teenager. "Lady Shia Ronin, I'd like for you to meet my sister, and her family. I certainly hope you're up for the task."

He opened his hand and moved it closer to her.

Shia shot him a glance, looked down at his hand, and then wrapped her fingers in his. She stole one more glance and felt comfort in his response. Ryan smiled and squeezed her fingers.

"We're standing at the crossroads where day and night divide,
It takes all of your heart to keep the light alive,
And the darkness seems so endless until the dawn arrives,
We'll hold the spark between us and keep the light alive."